for Ruth,
with fond memories
of Yugoland,
NYC, Dec 1997

BITTERSWEET

Phillip Corwin

MINERVA PRESS
MONTREUX LONDON WASHINGTON

BITTERSWEET

ISBN 1 85863 601 9

First published 1995 by
MINERVA PRESS
1 Cromwell Place,
London SW7 2JE

Printed in Great Britain by
B.W.D. Ltd., Northolt, Middlesex

BITTERSWEET

Acknowledgements

Ark River Review, City Paper, Contemporary American Satire, G. W. Review, Midstream, Mind In Motion, North Dakota Quarterly, Northeast, Pulpsmith, Quixote, Rampike Magazine, The Villager, West Wind Review.

CONTENTS

Not to want to say, not to know what you want to say, not to be able to say what you think you want to say, and never to stop saying, or hardly ever, that is the thing to keep in mind, even in the heat of composition.

Samuel Beckett

Damsel With Dulcimer

Spy I? rumbled Calhoun. Wherefore spy me? Impounded baggage why? Customs officials perpetrating crude customs. Government nuns with dirty habits.

WELCOME TO ADDIS ABABA, the sign at the airport terminal read. THIRTEEN MONTHS OF SUNSHINE, a poster added.

Lying, the poster. Outside raining. Sunshine by Socialist customs as yet uncleared no doubt. Unwelcoming. Unaccustomed. Terminal disease, this.

"Please stand over by the wall. Someone will come by shortly to forage your luggage," says a uniformed predator. 0630 hours, Sunday, June 1984. Sam Edward Calhoun, unwilling to put his back to the wall to be inspected, having flown all night from Rome after having waited three hours at the airport for an Ethiopian Air connection, and having started from New York eighteen long hours earlier, refuses.

"Wait a minute!" says he loudly. Stray carrion bags zip to attention. A few shoulder bags swell with hope. It is hot, dry. The air is thin because of the height of the city. Calhoun fears loss of all rights, including copyright. Thirsty.

"Can I talk at you?" addressed to the gaunt, young man who has just given the peremptory ordure, and who wears an olive drab shirt with torn epaulets. A lieutenant kernel perhaps, thinks Calhoun. Continuing: "I'm here for the food conference at the invitation of the Ethiopian Government," trying to sound authoritative. Thinking: why the hell else would I be here? "Can I bypass the heart of your customs and traditions? I have a reservation at the Axum Hotel (the one with the understated Orwellian decor). I've been flying all night and my wings are tired. Let me through or I'll tell your comrades you're Jewish."

"Someone will come by shortly to inspect your thoughts. Meanwhile, you'll have to stand over by the wall with the rest of the luggage and learn some slogans." The man's voice is very flat. He carries a walkie-talkie. He speaks into it in Amharic, and it answers in Leninism.

"But wait!" Calhoun persists. The man walks away. The terminal is small. There is only one baggage claim area, and that is small too.

Scores of people are waiting. Two armed guards stand at the only exit. WELCOME, the sign says.

Loudly curses he. Staring people. Acrid perspiration smells he of himself. Moldy, mephitic. Dizzy. Zipper jacket off. His damp shirt clings to his body like a wet suit. His gray corduroy slacks are wrinkled and creaseless from his having sat up all night on the plane. His undershorts ride up on him and are likewise damp, soggy, like a wad of cotton pressing up, grimy.

What here am I doing? asks he. To conference or not to conference, that is the tissue of the issue.

Walkie-talkies talking to one another crisscross the terminal. A banner hangs from the railing above the baggage claim area; it has a large five-pointed star inside a red circle with a hammer and sickle under the star.

What am doing here I? again to himself. Is escape ever? To a passing uniform: "Would you please show me the way to the time warp? I'm lost, and I came to save lives."

He sits on the floor, stretches his legs out full length, and tries to touch his spinning head to his knees. If I sleep I die, he imagines. Must exercise. Keep heart pumping, jumping. But pelvis unwilling, a clear case of bad management, Will not in control of Body. His disrespectful, wadded underwear chokes. Looks up. Staring people again. And again he curses, loudly.

Now he touches the soles of his feet together and presses on the insides of his knees with his elbows. Then hands behind orbiting head, legs outstretched again, left elbow to right knee, inquiring: Have you seen the twentieth century pass this way? I seem to have lost it. Right elbow to left knee, demanding: Take me to your leader's Commissar. I want Commissary privileges. Right to left, left to right. His stubborn, water-logged knees goose-step to interior chants. Meanwhile, disobedient taut and untaught lower back muscles bursting.

"Against the wall move please. You'll have to wait like the others, so that every class of baggage can be equally uncomfortable. Socialism has no class."

"But I'm not a groupie. I'm a dirty Western individualist! Besides, nobody wants to be with me because I'm unpatriotic; I ignore deodorant advertisements. Why can't we go through the line one at a time, me first, if I promise to say three Hail Lenins?"

"We have to inspect for electronic equipment. All must be searched at the same time."

"The guy sitting behind me on the trip from Rome was AC/DC. He's your man," says Calhoun.

"We are waiting for clearance from our superiors on the evolutionary scale and then you will be allowed to pass through." Departing, trailing 13 months of sunshine.

"But I'm special. I'm here at the invitation of your phantom Government. Let me through or I'll wreck your prisons and you won't have any place to board journalists. I'll have my Government de-caffeinate your Coca-Cola."

Ignored. More walkie-talkie talk. Probably 7-Uppers, Calhoun amuses.

Time passes. Sixty minutes or more. Calhoun's outblown head returns to his godly knees as he sits outstretched on the airport floor, intent on activating his heart. Heart-on! he commands. Then reflects: here doing am I what? Why the hell doing here am I? Suddenly: "Are you all right, sir?" The voice of a woman.

Head buried, he has not seen or heard her approach. Without uplooking he says: "I want to get out of here and go to my hotel. I've been flying all night and my arms are tired. I have a *Laissez Passer*." Unlocking knees.

"What nationality are you?" asks she.

He blanches beneath his sweat, swallows his swollen resistance, and regards his interlocutress. "American."

She is wearing a light blue two-piece suit, a white blouse and black shoes. There is an Ethiopian flag in her lapel. It is a uniform, but she gives it character. Her legs are streams of candied syrup poured from her narrow waist; he can see that, he can intuit that, even though her skirt comes well below her knees. Her eyes are a deep sienna brown, intense, limpid, endearing. And though her features seem strangely ageless, Calhoun estimates her to be about thirty. She is an Abyssinian cat, lissom and classic; a beauteous feline in this pack of bureaucratic turtles.

Rising, he records for posterity: In this air terminal for flying nightmares, this Halfway House for stray romantics wanting to rescue the needy, this arid bone in the throat of humanity, I have come to meet Shala. That is why I am here, and only why: Shala. For that was her name.

"I *thought* you were an American," says she, of dream stuff woven. "Perhaps I can help you." Her black hair fluffs about her shoulders. Her features are more Semitic than African. Quotes he: A damsel with a dulcimer/In a vision once I saw:/It was an Abyssinian maid,/And on her dulcimer she played.

"I'm here for the food conference," says he. "Where's your dulcimer and how did you get it through customs?"

"I *know* why you're here," she says.

"I don't normally talk to strange visions," continues he, heart-on pumping aerobically. "Can you play Melancholy Baby on your beautiful instrument, or are you just a mirage?"

"Get your luggage and come see me. I think I can help. I'll be waiting by the inspection station."

Obediently, he tugs at his luggage and comes. Whereupon quickly she clears him through customs and traditions while the others, backs to the wall, wait and watch and writhe and hug their frustrations. And then she takes him to his hotel in a Government limousine and finds him a suite even though the hotel has lost his reservation and is allegedly full. And then, without the slightest revelation of body or soul, she leaves. "I'll see you tomorrow at the conference," says she before he can reach for his Word Gun.

"Okay. Tomorrow."

* * * * *

Tomorrow and tomorrow and tomorrow come and go and sees he her. Night and day for the two weeks of the conference frequently see they each other. And the desert tongues wag and the bare walls watch and the Government officials cluck about this strange relationship between two people from different social systems, races and sexes.

And Calhoun sleeps alone and dreams of King Solomon. Here in Sheba Land where Solomon (when not dividing babies or promoting wisdom), had once plucked a beautiful young queen from her retinue and given her a prince, here he, Sam Edward Calhoun, forty and free floating, divorced and denuded of sexual restraint (he the peripatetic pursuer of urban princesses and defender of the great unwashed), has flown from across the sea to conference on food and gorge on resolutions while the distended bellies at the merciless African sun point and the voices of righteousness peddle petrodollars for protein.

In fact, Calhoun had come to Addis Ababa to write about the conference. He worked for one of the agencies in the United Nations family, and the Agency's Director of Information had dispatched Calhoun to assist in publicizing the conference and in determining the role that the Agency might play in feeding the hungry children of Africa.

Upon returning, Calhoun was to report on the prospects for inter-Agency nepotism, organizational incest and chauvinistic cannibalism in the afflicted regions of sub-Saharan Africa.

Meanwhile, during his lunch hours Calhoun counted eucalyptus trees and revered ancient Coptic churches, concluding that if every starving Ethiopian were to devour thirteen eucalyptus leaves each day - one for each month of sunshine, according to the Julian calendar - then the Church would bless itself and the Government could branch out into leaf franchises.

Moreover, because of the medicinal properties of eucalyptus he posited, no Ethiopian who perished from hunger would have to die again from respiratory disease. That would not only avoid having to suffer the indignity of dying twice (without even being reborn), but would also prevent unnecessary verbiage in coroner's reports, which in turn would save paper; and since paper came from trees, trees could be preserved to produce more eucalyptus leaves which indigenous indigents could ingest so that they would be able to die from malnutrition instead of respiratory disease.

Calhoun called this cycle a natural escho-system; in other words, an eschatological system that would limit death to starvation except in cases where there was enough to eat, and would allow degraded people to die with uninfected lungs.

As for Shala, she was there to provide aid and comfort. She was there on the job when Calhoun needed documents, statistics, appointments with delegations, tourist information, and even once, a physician. In the evenings, she escorted him to Ethiopian restaurants where they dined on prisoners of war.

One night, at dinner, she asked him if he would like to visit some collective farms in the south of Ethiopia during his last weekend in Addis. The Government was offering a tour for conference participants. She was going as a guide and would like him to come. It would be the Sunday after the conference was scheduled to end.

"No," he said. They were sitting in a room by themselves in a restaurant at the edge of Addis. What doing here am I? Calhoun had been asking himself again the last two nights. Now a collective she proposes? Is she pulling my humorous bone? The only collective he had ever considered seriously was guilt.

"I would rather go to Gondar or Lalibela or Axum," he said. They're in the opposite direction. "I'm interested in Ethiopian history."

"But you won't be able to go north," she said. "In the rainy season the airplanes can't always land, and the roads are closed because of the rebellions in Tigray and Eritrea. And there aren't any flights out of Addis until Monday. It's either spend Sunday in Addis or visit the collectives." The waitress had brought their *mesob*. It was a wicker basket, table height, shaped like an hour glass and covered. Shala removed the top. Inside was a tray filled with food.

"Why should I go to see the glories of collectivism?" he said. "I might as well stay in bed and count my vaccinations."

"Because I want you go come along." On the tray were stacked several slices of *ingera*, a pancake-shaped spongy bread, about eighteen inches in diameter. In the center of the *ingera* was a soft, watery cheese. On top of the cheese was *wat*, a soup almost like a sauce. Tonight because they were having *dorowat* (chicken soup), the sauce had pieces of chicken in it. It was not too spicy, in deference to Calhoun's sensitive American stomach, though usually *wat* was very hot.

"What's in it for me if I come along? Interviews with a few socialist roosters? A rap session with contented cows? Udder nonsense."

"A look at Ethiopian agriculture."

He reached for her hand. How romantic the prospect of a cowbarn in summer: a proletarian pastoral with sermons on egg production; flies buzzing about the ears; arid earth; tropical sun; fraternal solidarity with dung heaps; and not even a beach umbrella. In North Carolina, where he had been born and raised before dissipating to New York, a white man could get lynched for frolicking with a black girl in the summer hay. "Why are you spending so much time with me?" he interjected. "Almost every night we have dinner together. During the day you come by several times to see if I need help."

"I told you. My brothers are in Moscow studying. My sister is at home caring for my mother. I don't have a man to go home to since my husband died in the war in the Ogaden, and I don't have many chances to meet Americans. As for the conference, it's my job to help you."

"I don't believe you."

"What don't you believe?"

"I don't believe that's why you're spending so much time with me." Must be a practical reason, thought he. Must be she knows how easily I can be manipulated by ex-wives, thinking of his own X-rated wife, and the fact that Shala, too, was an ex-wife by virtue of a Somali bullet. Or maybe it's something specific she's after, like contraband cocoa from Kenya, because she has extra marshmallows that she doesn't want to waste while the conference delegates are glutting themselves with Ethiopian coffee. After all, who ever heard of a double espresso with marshmallows? Then again asking: What here am I the hell doing? And why am I so entranced with this descendant of Sheba, knowing full well the high risk situation inherent at such estrogen levels?

"What are you thinking?" she said.

"I think you've been assigned to watch me. I'm the only American at the conference and you're watching me. You told me at the airport that first day that you *knew* why I was here. Your Government assumed that I had come to spy, but instead you've been spying on me. Why else would you have singled me out from all those passengers that first day at the terminal? You were assigned to me."

She tore a bite-sized piece of *ingera* from the rim, and with her deft fingers scooped cheese and chicken sauce into the center, then rolled the bread into a pancake. Then she offered the food to Calhoun. "Open your mouth. This is called *gursha*," she said. "It's a tradition of feeding someone else. Sometimes a host will feed his guest this way. Sometimes a wife feeds her husband this way. It's a sign of respect or affection. The women are usually the ones who do the feeding because they are in charge of the food."

He opened his mouth and took the perfectly bite-sized offering. Then he helped himself to more. At the rim of the *ingera* were cooked vegetables and whole pieces of chicken - breasts, legs and wings. He tried to roll a small pancake for Shala, but could not, and he was embarrassed by the clumsiness of his Western fingers.

She rolled him another pancake, and he kissed her fingers as she placed the food in his mouth. Hungry was he. "I would ask you to come to my place for a party, but I know this is a one-Party State, and I don't want you to lose your only uniform. This may sound chicken, just because we're winging it, but we're already in the soup together, and if I kidnap you they would consider it a capitalist offence. What I'm trying to say is that no Ethiopian girl spends this much time with an American unless the Government assigns her," he insisted.

"Are you thirsty?" she asked. "They have a kind of home-made beer here called *tela*. The owner makes it himself in his cellar."

"Yes, I want some *tela* and I want you to tell me if you were assigned to spy on me. If not by the Government, then perhaps by my ex-wife who wants more alimony because my financial situation has worsened since I've grown up."

She rolled him another pancake. He ate it. "Yes," she said.

Once again his fingers fumbled as he tried to roll a neat pancake. Failing, he scooped chicken, vegetables, cheese and cabbage into a fistful of bread and, as gracefully as possible, stuffed it into his mouth. He felt as though he were shoveling coal into a furnace, his stomach having transformed itself from a junk pit into a furnace not many years ago. "You mean, yes, you were sent to spy on me?"

"Yes."

"But why? I have no secrets, I'm not an important official. I'm even willing to wear underwear made in the Third World if it will help sell washing machines made in America. I dutifully abandoned my incentive before joining the United Nations so that I wouldn't set a bad example for my colleagues. Why I? Wherefore spy me? What's *wat*?"

"I was supposed to report on you, whatever you did and said that might be interesting."

"To whom?"

"To my superior."

"Mother Superior? But this is an atheist country. I thought there was nun of that."

"Yes, to my superior. It doesn't matter who he is. Everybody spies on everybody else here."

"Have I given you enough to report?"

The *tela* arrived. The waitress poured them each a glass. Shala sipped. She was wearing the same two-piece blue suit, white blouse and black shoes she had been wearing when Calhoun arrived. She had worn the very same outfit every day. The top two button holes on her blouse were frayed. "You know," she said, ignoring his question, "I have a cousin in California who always asks me to visit him. There are a lot of Ethiopians in California."

"I didn't know that," he said. Her hair was clean and black and thick and beautiful. He touched it. He didn't want to talk politics. He hated politics. He wanted to talk about her. "How can you stand this petty espionage?" he asked.

She winced, and at once he was sorry he'd asked. For here was a woman who had lost her husband in a war, whose brothers had been forced into alien "study" in Moscow, and who was extremely fortunate to have a steady job, a place to live and enough to eat. "I'm sorry I asked," he said.

"I don't mind answering. I stand it because eventually I hope it will get me what I want."

"I understand." And of course he was sure that he did.

"No, you don't." And of course he didn't.

"One has to survive. *Il faut gagner sa croute*, as the French say."

"No, that's not it. That's not it at all. Surviving isn't hard. What I want is to defect."

He gagged and looked around. Help! he whispered to the nearest chicken wing. But said nothing, nothing. Now at last it was clear which *wat* was what. Chicken was not the same as sacrificial lamb.

"You must help me."

Deep breath. Then some *tela*. "I'm leaving in a few days, there's nothing I can do. I'll get you all the marshmallows you want, but you're on your own when it comes to cocoa."

"You must help me. You can approach the American officials. You know what must be done. I know from the inside something about how the Ethiopian Government operates. I can be of use."

He fumbled with the *ingera* again but his fingers were even clumsier than before. "How do I know you're not just trying to set me up? Tomorrow I could get arrested and be thrown into an Ethiopian jail for trying to lure a defector to the West. No. I can't be sure what you really want. Anyway, we shouldn't talk like this here."

"It's all right here. It's private. And don't worry, you don't have to do anything to help me until after you leave Ethiopia. Then you will know what to do. Please! You're the only American I know. I can't ask a perfect stranger for something like this."

He thrust his hands into the *wat* and tried to think of several whos. Obviously, when and how were not as important as why. Wherefore I? thought he.

"Trust me," she said. "I'll come to see you at your hotel Sunday night after I return from the tour and we'll talk."

"Okay. Sunday night."

* * * * *

Eagerly awaited he her. Storms gathering in and out, and Calhoun abed. Familiar, this: woman waiting.

What the penalty for defection? he wondered. Was complicity always criminal? Or could it be civil, a tort, as in torture? And why he? Wherefore spy I? Punning punster punished, would the headlines hawk. Descendant of Sheba she-boomed along with alien unintelligence agent. No impunity for civil savants.

Terrible this tyranny against the personal. The Government not allowing nationals to visit the hotel rooms of foreigners. A curfew clearing the windswept streets by midnight. Where to make love, a human rite?

She entered the hotel compound hooded, like an Iranian, wrapped in a disguise to make her look like a night servant, mumbling in Amharic, shrewd enough to make herself anonymous, a gift of the Magi. Then around to the rear of the hotel and through an outdoor corridor lit only by the full moon, until she reached Calhoun's building, shrouded by eucalyptus trees and dancing in shadows as the rain clouds floated across the June sky. "Shala," she said, gently rapping, rapping on his chamber door.

There was a large, open courtyard between his suite and the main building where the receptionist was located, and when it rained it was virtually impossible to cross the courtyard. The wind thrashed, the bouganvilla swayed menacingly and the pebbles and gravel stacked neatly in piles swirled and shot through the air like lethal pellets. At such times the rain cascaded in hard drops, mud spattered and splashed against the white stucco buildings, and dozens of insects washed into the dirt paths, soggy, heavy and very dead.

He could feel that the storm would begin any minute now. And then it would be difficult for her to leave until the storm had ended. He opened the door for her, and she wafted in on the spume of his imagination gracefully, silently, magically. "Did you have any trouble getting into the compound?" he asked.

"No," unwrapping her shawl and throwing it over a chair. "Look, I've brought you this." It was a painting on goat skin, a panel about three feet long and a foot wide that was rolled up like a scroll. Indigenous art, unlike anything he had ever seen before coming to Ethiopia. There were five pictures, and writing under each in Amharic. "It's the story of Solomon and Sheba," she said.

"But why are you gifting me when you are the gift?"

"I want you to remember Ethiopia."

"I may not be leaving so fast. I haven't even seen the jails yet." Gulping air, he approached and began to unwrap her, his unanticipated gift. Being baited he, surely in the hands of a skillful masterbaiter. Outside wind battered the roof tiles and a few large drops pummeled the stucco. Ached he throughout. Fingertips dancing. Kissing her as she talked of Sheba and Menilek I and the Solomonic dynasty. His tyrannical curiosity swelling and she warmly responding to each probing question. Oh, how much she knew!

"If I could only get to America I could live with my cousin in California."

"Shall I pack you in my suitcase? What are you asking?"

"No one is free until everyone is free."

"I'm not who you think I might be. I'm not even sure myself who I am."

"I have nothing here. You have everything there."

"I could get hanged by my passport for violating your curfew. You're not even supposed to be in this hotel now, let alone in California."

"All I'm asking for is your nationality. You don't have to marry me. Girls like to have fun too. Besides, what you do after you leave Ethiopia will only be between you and your conscience."

"But I didn't bring my conscience with me. It's with my mother in North Carolina. She keeps it locked in a wall safe. Sometimes she lends it to me when I'm threatened with a serious relationship, but otherwise I leave it with her. It's too much responsibility to have it around all the time. I wouldn't want to lose it. You only get one each lifetime, like virginity."

"But at least you own one. I knew that the first time I saw you at the airport."

"Aha! Maybe that's what the official officials were really looking for when they were going through everyone's luggage. Heavy-duty consciences pay heavy duties."

"Maybe," she said.

"Then I'm glad I didn't bring mine along. It would have only got me in trouble. It takes terrible advantage of me when I carry it; it's bossy, righteous, nosy. That's why I like to leave it behind when I travel to other dimensions. I can be much more spontaneous without it."

"Anyhow, conscience or not, I still have faith in you."

"Shows bad judgment, very bad judgment."

"Why?"

"Because I'm not always faithful. And you shouldn't ask me to be faithful already. We're not even lovers yet."

"You're very funny."

"Come here," he said. "I want to see if you're wired for sound. I'd hate to think that what I thought I was saying in private was really pubic. And he dropped to the ground and turned her around to search her for sound.

"What are you singing?" she asked as she danced. "I like your rhythm."

"*California Bound*," he answered.

And the big drops hammered the thick air and the heavy windows shook and the precarious dim lights in the corridors went out.

"I am a pirate. I am a cannibal. I am a hostage," thought Calhoun, hugging his goatskin.

* * * * *

Airport taxes attacked the heavily taxed as the taxis taxied to the taxers next morning at the terminal. Quaked, unearthly Calhoun.

"I'll pay. I know it's my duty," cried he to every uniform on duty. "Better duty than booty."

"Have you anything to declare?" said an official official as Calhoun lined up to stand in line. The man was a pock-marked, pigeon-toed captain in his thirties, with a hoarse voice.

"I declare my innocence. I came here to conference on food and now I feel stuffed with rhetoric. I can't gorge any more on arid land or feast on famine. If you want to search my luggage, it's all right, but I assure you I left my conscience at home."

"How did you like Addis Ababa? It's my home town. I've starved here all my life."

"It's far better as political capital than starving children. I don't think starving children should be used as political capital."

"Are you bringing any gifts home with you?"

"Aside from Shala, only Solomon and Sheba," unrolling his painted painting.

"Where exactly in America do you live?"

"Really, wherever my mind takes me. I have family infections in North Carolina, an apartment in New York, and a damsel with a dulcimer about to arrive in California. Do you know that poem about a damsel with a dulcimer?"

"Sir, we have three wars going on now, not counting the one against our own past, and I'm a captain in the people's army, which is fighting a war against the people. That's why we have thirteen months in the Ethiopian calendar, so that we can fit in all the wars. How do you expect me to find time for poetry?"

"I know exactly how you feel," said Calhoun. "Poets are dangerous anyway. They always want us to lay down our arms, but I have a long flight to New York, and if I laid down my arms I'd never get off the ground."

"Are you flying with Ethiopian Air?"

"At the start, of course. After all, I can't very well fly in a vacuum, even if it would be cleaner. But I'll be using my arms whenever possible to help steer, which is why I can't be expected to lay them down, or even to keep them in my lap."

"I see," said the captain. "'Forewarned is forearmed', as they say. I'm glad you enjoyed Ethiopia."

"I enjoyed it so much that I'll be taking a beautiful sample home with me after I leave."

"You will?"

"Yes. I gave my word. And I have to keep it."

And Sam Edward Calhoun did, in fact, keep his word. For he knew full well that it was his most valued possession, that it was he himself; knowing that in the beginning was his word, at the end would be his word, and in between was his Word Gun; more human, he or anyone else could never be.

And one year later Shala came to California.

And Calhoun wrote a story about her.

* * * * *

1992

Coca

At the first meeting of The Society, every single person that had been invited came alone and left together.

The guest lecturer was a lawyer formerly specializing in prenuptual agreements and now concentrating on post-coital nihilism. Her name was Coca.

Coca was an international celebrity and a literary luminary. She had first come to prominence by writing the biography of an obscure Colombian Air Force General as seen through the eyes of a coca leaf. ("He plucked me as soon as I was ripe, ground me to paste in his jungle hideaway and sold me to an international syndicate that abused me repeatedly. But I loved him." Etc.) The critics, the publishers, the entire academic establishment adored her.

At her lecture to The Society, she wore a gold cross around her neck and a movable set of resplendent fangs attached to her knees. She spoke about hostages. Emotional attachments, she had learned through compulsive experience, made one a hostage. Pre-emotional attachments made one vulnerable to being taken hostage. Love absolutely destroyed the immune system.

Her lecture was riveting. I remember it well because I was seated apart from a total stranger on the other side of the room who was one day to become my ex-wife. If only, Coca had said, we could gain knowledge without experience, wisdom without age, or enlightenment without taxes, then we could attain whatever we desired.

Years later when I was trying every depilatory known to medicine in order to detach myself from a woman I was about to meet, Coca's words came back to me, and I realized how prescient she had been.

She has also been successful financially. Her lectures are now video taped, packaged, and sold at outrageous prices. I realize I should have collected her literary droppings from the start; but, alas, hindsight is always clearer than foresight, just as hindskin is always tougher than foreskin.

Meanwhile, on that memorable night as I listened to Coca, my bones rattled with excitement. And when the lights in the auditorium dimmed and she stood spotlighted on that small proscenium stage, she looked as though she had just stepped out of a painting by Willem de Kooning. She had style and wit and fangs, and obviously practiced what she preached. I had never seen such a model of molecular biology.

She spoke about the trap of loneliness, and how it might tempt one into daring a relationship that could only end in lawyer's fees. She spoke about the trap of sex and how it could only end in blood tests and long-term educational debentures. She spoke about the trap of companionship and how it could only end in competition.

She had amazing insights. She had amazing grace. She had an amazing trap.

As soon as she had finished her lecture I offered to be her business manager.

"Yes," she said. "I can see how we might be able to use each other ruthlessly."

Her choice of words was not fortuitous. When Coca was a baby her mother had always called her "Baby Ruth"; and although Coca insisted that name-calling had had absolutely no influence on her pre-coital development, the fact was that she had hated her baby name so much that she vowed to be ruthless if she ever matured.

Intent only on business, I assured her that I had absolutely nothing attractive to offer so far as a personal relationship was concerned. A woman would have to be kinky to be interested in me.

She made a brief comment about the trap of kinkiness, and how it could only end in normality. Then she agreed that I should become her business manager.

She insisted on an escape clause ("escape claws", she wrote) in our contract that would allow either party to withdraw spontaneously and without penalty at the first sign of real or imagined sentiment for the opposite party, a third party, or him/herself. Since we were both athletes (not to be a member of a health club at that time was considered unpatriotic), she insisted that we could only engage in individual sports like jogging, swimming, skiing, hot coal walking or self-effacement, but not in group sports like marriage, politics, soccer or bridge-building.

"You got it, Baby Ruth," I said through my attorney, who was seated in an adjacent room, apart from either of us at the signing.

"Cool, Fool," she responded tenderly.

We immediately began with a world-wide tour of religious institutions in order to establish credibility with the American people. The clergy loved Coca. They understood instantly her scheme to exploit human desperation and misery. Coca grew to be revered. Several hagiographers received six-figure advances from publishers interested in the story of her life. We made big bucks.

I must explain, meanwhile, in order to avoid confusion, that whenever Coca appeared at religious functions she was known as "Candy". That was because a certain corporation which owned and leased numerous pulpits and did extensive preaching insisted that Coca's name threatened to compete with its own classic product. On that basis, the Coalition of the Churches of America (acronym: COCA) agreed to refer to Coca as "Candy", which derived from her childhood nickname.

For several months, the money flowed in. It was like 'stealing candy from a baby', Coca said ruthlessly. But then, after being constantly on the road, with no permanent home to return to for abuse, I became restless. Perhaps I had a crisis of faith, perhaps I didn't like churches, perhaps I didn't like candy. I don't know. Whatever the reason, I suggested to Coca that we should change our lifestyles. We needed a different audience, a challenge, I told her. Besides, our profitability had peaked.

She didn't care what we did. She was totally detached.

What ideas did she have, I asked. Video tapes? Books? Cosmetic endorsements? Frozen jello sculptures?

"Use your head, Sucka," she replied. "Just take care of business."

I reminded her that I was only asking for her opinion.

"If you had any brains, Snake, you'd know without asking! The best things in life carry no obligation."

(Under the terms of our contract, and in keeping with American family tradition, we were obligated, whenever talking, to insult each other constantly in order to preclude the insidious formation of any affection.)

"Maybe we should start addressing lawyers' groups," I proposed. Our message of profiting from detachment was just what they needed.

"Waste of time - they wrote the original script."

"What about doctors?" I asked.

"Nothing there either, Dummy. They're high-tech bankers, as soon cut you as cash your check. Besides, the malpractice insurance companies have that market sewed up: you can already sue for malpractice at any sign of compassion. The whole heart transplant business was a test run for implanting feelings in emotional robots."

"Sometimes I don't know what the hell you're talking about," I said.

"Then praise me and become a literary critic, Mindless."

"What about economists?" I resumed. "Good potential for conversion."

"Ever try to convert a Polish zloty?"

"What about politicians? You frigid bitch," I cooed.

"Like pouring perfume down a toilet bowl, you epicene egoist. They'd take our message and run with it. No market there."

"Maybe we could try speaking again at The Society, where we first met. That was inspiring."

"The first meeting there was the last meeting. I thought you knew that."

I became distraught. I told her I wanted to terminate our business relationship.

"We have no relationship," she reminded me, "only a contract."

"That's the point," I said. "Our contract may be *in*valid."

"You mean in*val*id."

"No, I mean *in*valid, as in 'sick'."

"Who? What? How? When? Where and why?"

"Let me explain. Do you know the fable about the fox and the grapes?"

"Yes, of course," she said.

"Well, that has nothing to do with what I'm about to say."

"I see."

"I know what the problem is. We can't continue the way we are because...because I'm (laughing)...I'm falling in love with you."

"@#$%&*."

"I *knew* you'd understand."

She started laughing too. "I can't help myself," she said.

"And I have to help myself because nobody else will."

"It's inevitable, don't you see?"

"What is?"

"Falling in love."

"So is dying. So are taxes."

"So is laughter."

She looked at me. "Haven't you been listening to my lectures?" she asked.

"Yes, of course, but I wasn't paying attention."

"You need protection. Your mass is becoming critical."

"I'm in pain, that's the problem."

"You must be getting old."

"Older," I said.

She turned ashen. The blood seemed to drain from her body. "I'm very unattractive. When you look at me, you're not seeing what you think you see."

"Love is blind."

"You may not feel tomorrow the same as you feel today. And today you might not feel the same as you did yesterday."

"Love is timeless."

She seemed to grow weaker and thinner before my very eyes.

"Please stop this foolishness. Please!"

"You're hiding something," I said.

"I'm hiding everything," she said. And vaporized in a matter of seconds.

There is not much more to tell except to say that I never saw Coca alive again after that.

Months passed. I brooded, recovered and began to search for her, but she was nowhere to be found. I placed an advertisement in the "Personals" column of several sex magazines. I hired a defective detective. I used ouija boards. I tried cursing in iambic pentameter; but I received no response. Coca seemed gone forever.

Then one evening I returned to The Society. It was twilight. There was no one there except for a security guard who had a bone through his nose. I went to the lecture hall and meditated. And after what seemed like an eternity, and I was just about to leave, I suddenly had a vision of Coca at the lectern, gold cross around her neck and movable set of resplendent fangs attached to her knees.

I stood up and walked toward her. But the closer I came the more she faded. By the time I reached the lectern she had vanished.

"Baby Ruth!" I called to the darkness.

No answer.

"All right, Coca. Now hear this, wherever you are: I don't love you any longer. You're free."

Still no answer.

"And I never did love you."

But there was only silence and a slight echo. I could feel my thoughts ricochet against my lips. I turned and left.

And the next night, after making sure that the security guard would be able to escape unharmed, I burned The Society to the ground.

* * * * *

1991

One World

(This story, originally published as an excerpt, is the opening section of an unpublished novel entitled *A Matter of Murder*.)

It is October 1973. There is war again in the Middle East.

I am thousands of miles away on the other side of the globe, at an office in New York City, but the shells are falling around me. Armored battalions roll across my skin; I am an armadillo. My throat is the Sinai Desert. My thoughts are trapped somewhere on the Golan Heights, mortally threatened by the thump thump of artillery. I can hear screams, pleas for mercy, in five languages.

Am I losing my mind? Why should I care if the world burns? What fate could be more deserved? I stroll to the water cooler, flaunting my security and non-involvement, my freedom; I depress the pedal and a curious mixture of oil and blood arcs onto my tongue. My alimentary canal is but a tributary to the Suez.

* * * * *

The One World Organization, for which I am privileged to work, is the largest intergovernmental organization on the planet, with offices in over seventy five countries and headquarters in New York City, Geneva, Vienna and Nairobi. Every day distinguished representatives meet in our hallowed halls for the twin purposes of beating swords into plowshares and legislating morality. Of course they have been unable to do either as yet; but then, no organization in recorded history has been able to pacify mankind's murderous instincts, so that One World is no more of a failure than most schemes for realizing the Good have been. Everything is relative. Think on it: the fires of hell are only hot if you are not accustomed to living there.

How I came to work here is a long story, and I shall tell it to you. But I must warn you at the start that, for all the acid in my veins, I am a believer; not a crusader, not a proselytizer, not a missionary, but a believer...in love, humanity, justice, joy - joy most of all, even if I haven't always had enough of it. And so if you are looking for someone who will throw muck at the world and tell you how corrupt and imperfect humanity is, well, there will be some of that here, because that, too, is a part of the truth. But remember that even excrement, according to the laws of the universe, regenerates. Yes, if you want me again look for me under your bootsoles, as Whitman said.

Have you ever read cosmology? Oh, you must read cosmology for we are, indeed, *star stuff* as the cosmologists insist. The atoms that make you and me were formed billions of years ago in an astonishing cosmic fireball that created time itself. Somewhere out there in the intergalactic hydrogen clouds are our ancestors. And somewhere out there, perhaps, are our progeny, or at least, our future neighbors. What is distance anyhow? What are billions of light years? Even time is but an extension of space, and if one could travel fast enough, approaching light speed, he might even discover the future.

* * * * *

My colleagues are from almost every country in the world. I do not have to travel to Capetown, Minsk, Jaipur, Montevideo, Tasmania, Bali, Canton, Zagreb, Aden, Kinshasa, Quito, Accra or Ouagadougou to meet them. They are here. There is even a woman down the hall who comes from Brooklyn.

But this morning my visitors are from the Soviet Union. They are a Russian, a Ukrainian and a Georgian, as different from one another as bears from balalaikas - yet in some ways as similar as three offset prints from the same official mat. They are my constant companions. I call them the Marx Brothers.

The Russian is the first to visit. His name is Ivan Slutzkin. He is in his middle forties, possessed of a very good sense of humor, astute and obscene. He has a small torso and long arms that seem to hang to his knees, and when he walks he rolls from side to side on the balls of his feet like a sailor. He has the movement of a fat man except that he is thin. "Good morning, Ilyusha," he says to me. My name is Elliot Hart. He calls me Ilyusha sometimes as a tease.

"Good morning, comrade," I say.

"How are you today?"

"Wonderful. How are you?"

"Equally wonderful. Tip top, as you Americans say."

"That's nice."

An uneasy pause. A painted smile. Eyes directly into mine. And then suddenly I know that something controversial is coming and I have a vision, the most xenophobic and racist of visions, but nonetheless stark and, I am sure, devilishly accurate. I see a troika materializing in Slutzkin's mind, slushing its way through the labyrinthine whorls of his pan-Slavic brain, each convolution a century of turbulent tradition. Slutzkin himself is seated in the sleigh, Rasputin is driving, and the three beasts in harness are composites, spiritual conglomerates, multi-layered avatars of Russian legend. One beast is Lenin, Stalin, Trotsky, Bakunin, *et al.*, a violent, hydra-headed prince of political idealism; the second beast is a blend of czars reaching back over five centuries, garlanded with roses and coughing blood, and the third, the beast in the middle, is the Grand Inquisitor.

I am often plagued by such visions when I converse with Soviets. It is as though I can never see them one - or even two - dimensionally. I always see through and behind them; each face I imagine to be a fresco of centuries of suffering, of an accursed history of oppression and violence, sentimentality and stoicism, seditious ambition and thwarted political nationalism; they are all children of an unhappy marriage between East and West. In no other people has there been such a passionate clash between pagan mysticism and religious orthodoxy, between peasant superstition and European rationalism, between democratic yearnings and feudal corruption. I am drawn to their culture, yet I fear them. They are the greatest revolutionaries of all, yet they have never had a revolution. Indeed, the great October Revolution was nothing more than another turn of the screw, another twist on the torture rack of the Russian experience.

In any case, my vision fades and Slutzkin is there facing me with his eminently practical conversation. He has come to visit me in order to collect information; his mission has a purpose. And no sooner does he make known his purpose than my worst suspicions are confirmed, and my most guarded beliefs are vilely exposed in a pogrom of privacy. "Tell me, Elliot, what do you think of this war your people have started? It may not go so good this time, you know."

The fact is that I am both an American and a Jew, and am constantly under attack for being either or both. This time it is the Jew who is being fired upon. By "your people" Slutzkin has meant the Jews. It is no matter that both Egypt and Syria chose to cross cease-fire lines and fired first at the Israelis to begin the October war of 1973. Nor does it matter that I am not an Israeli. To Slutzkin, the Jews - the Jews all over the world, not just the Israelis - have started this war, just as they have started or been responsible for every war for the past century, including both world wars (in order to profit financially, and advance the cause of world Zionism), and they must be confronted whenever possible with their crimes.

I am astonished by Slutzkin's question, even though I had anticipated some form of frontal assault. And part of my astonishment is because of my casual attitude toward being Jewish. In New York City, being Jewish is no great distinction. Actually, I am an atheist, do not believe in theocracies, and have never been to Israel. But during the three years that I have been working for One World, I have been Jew-baited more than ever before in my life. It is something I simply don't understand. "I have no idea what you're talking about," I say to Slutzkin.

"Oh, come on, come on!. You people are always so shrewd! You know what I'm talking about," he says.

"Not a clue."

"The war! The war the Jews started so that they could acquire more territory."

"It's not my war, schmuck! Why don't you ask an Arab about it?"

A glint of satisfaction in his rotten eyes: he has provoked me. "This must be a time of great tension for you. I can understand that. But what will you do?"

"What will you do?" I reply, not knowing what else to say short of cursing his ancestry; and at the same time, not exactly sure what he means.

"Will you volunteer?"

"For what?" astonished.

"To go to Israel. I've heard that many Jews from all over the world are volunteering to go to Israel to help with the war effort."

"Are you recruiting?"

"Ah! Very funny. You people have a good sense of humor."

Pause. He is still smiling. I am amazed how well prepared he seems for this little interrogation. He seems to have been rehearsed, prompted, coached. It is as though he is going through a checklist of questions. "Well?" he says.

"Well, what?"

"Are you going to Israel?"

"You must be kidding...I live in New York...I have a job...I'm an American...I'm not going anywhere; I don't know what the hell you're talking about!"

"Then perhaps you'll send money if you won't go yourself."

"Perhaps I'll kill a Russian in New York if I can't get one in the Sinai Desert. Perhaps that's what I'll do."

"Oh, Ilyusha," he responds quickly, never at a loss for political repartees, "don't be silly. We are on your side. We are your friends. We like the Jews. Do you think we trust the goddamed Arabs? We only want the Zionists to give up the territories they captured in 1967, so that there will be peace in the area. Tension in the Mediterranean is no good for anyone. Once Israel returns to the 1967 boundaries, the Soviet Union will guarantee Israel's right to exist. Don't forget, the Soviet Union supported the establishment of Israel in 1948."

"If you'd get your asses out of the Mediterranean, there wouldn't be any tension."

His smile fades, then quickly returns as a sneer. I have stung him, and this time he attacks me for being an American. "Why should we get out of the Mediterranean?" he says. "Why should the Mediterranean be an American lake? Why not a Russian lake? You Americans are only using the Jews as an excuse for keeping your military bases in the Mediterranean. No, no, we are not so stupid as you think. We must protect our borders. You will not throw us out of the Mediterranean."

My resolve hardens and a phalanx of well-reasoned arguments lines up from one end of my tongue to the other. *Borders*! Since when did the borders of the Soviet Union extend to the Golan Heights and the Sinai Desert? I contemplate arguing with him, I fantasize humiliating him intellectually. I am prepared to take the offensive, to quote Marx and Lenin as often as he, and to prove by dialectical argument that he is being a left-wing opportunist or some such heretical deviationist. I know my Marxism and I know his soft points, from the 1939 alliance with Hitler to the exile of Solzhenitsyn. But then all at once I look again into his taunting eyes and my anger overwhelms my logic. "Ivanovich, fuck you," I say, well aware that I am virtually conceding defeat by retreating into such inelegant imprecations.

"Ah, Ilyusha, you are angry. I didn't mean to make you angry. I am only concerned that your people are doing such a foolish thing, and that you shouldn't waste your own money by donating it to buy weapons and by supporting imperialism."

"I didn't realize you were an investment adviser, comrade." Back to being a Jew, it seems, after briefly having been an American with designs on the Mediterranean.

"You must realize that Zionism is doomed, Ilyusha. You're not a fool. You're probably not even a Zionist! Zionism doesn't represent you. Look at it sensibly. How can a few million Jews overpower 120 million Arabs, even with American weapons? The only solution is to live in peace, to give back the captured territories and then a final settlement will be possible."

At this point I have another vision. I see Slutzkin attending a 7 a.m. briefing at the Soviet Mission this morning. Menu: eggs, toast, tea and propaganda. No one is allowed to leave the table until he has memorized his script. Assignment: to confront all available Jews and try to convince them of the foolishness of their position; also to record their reactions and report back to the Mission so that an effective strategy may be developed for undermining Zionist influence in the United States. "I have a better idea," I say. "Why not put the occupied territories in escrow with the Central Committee of the Soviet Communist Party until the Arabs and the Israelis learn to live together in peace - which will be never. How would that be?"

He sighs. "No, we don't want other people's territory. You don't seem to realize; we're on your side. We have a large Jewish population in the Soviet Union and it has great influence. We could never be anti-Jewish. We like our Jews. We need our Jews."

My teeth are prison bars, my words are convicted felons.

He goes on: "All right, Ilyusha. I understand. You're not volunteering and you're reluctant to send any of your own funds. I think that is wise." And then he turns to leave, his polling apparently completed.

"Would you like me to sign a memo to that effect?"

"No, it's okay," perfectly serious.

"*Heil*, Brezhnev," I say, rising from my desk and clicking my heels.

"*Hail*, Nixon...and that Jew Kissinger too," he says.

"You're an abomination!" I cry out suddenly. And I am embarrassed by the force of my voice, virtually humiliated by the brutish, deep-seated hatred I feel at that moment.

But Slutzkin merely laughs and continues on down the hall, rolling from side to side in his simian gait, seeking out the next Jew.

* * * * *

1982

O'Kay

for L.W.H.

You can imagine the consternation among the citizens of the People's Democratic Republic of O'Kay when their government decided to abolish language.

A heated, non-verbal debate ensued. Those who opposed the ruling said it would be an evolutionary regression. Moreover, the Word Gang (as they came to be known) maintained that knowledge once acquired by a species could not easily be unlearned. Once having learned to walk, for example, it would be virtually impossible to unlearn walking - not to mention jogging, broad jumping, disco dancing, soccer, aerobics and footsy.

Those who favored abolishing language, meanwhile, asserted it would lead to an advanced form of communication, such as ESP or LSD. This group became known as the Sounders, named after certain aquatic mammals who use sonar devices in lieu of language, and who, incidentally, have been around for longer than humans and don't kill one another for political reasons.

To deal with the crisis, several private societies were formed, and several public interest groups were malformed.

There was some question, of course, as to what actually constituted language, oral as well as written. Some confused it with communication, believing that grunts, bloodthirsty oaths, or mating calls could actually be construed as language. But the Supreme Court of the Republic eventually made a distinction amongst sound, language and government decrees. The Court's ruling came in a dense, 50,000-word document which adduced why language could no longer be relied on for communication. In fact, after the Court's decision was made public, the Leader was heard to say, "In the beginning was the Word, at the end was the Court."

Historians, who had also been abolished, termed the Court's judgment "the supreme enigmatic word enema", making a play on the word "supreme".

The Court, for its part, cited a statement once made by a famous American behavioral psychologist, the founder of modern advertising, who said: "Human thought processes are only motor movements in the larynx."

Following the Court's ruling, laryngitis was considered a gift of the gods.

(Gods, incidentally, were also abolished, although gifts, especially to high public officials, were not.)

For months following the Court's decree, no one spoke. The parents of small children were overjoyed. Publishers, who were already heavily involved in garbage recycling and distribution, became sanitation consultants and improved their ethics. Grammarians continued to be ignored, and national awards were established for functional illiteracy.

Then one day the Leader and the Ruling Council received a written letter which, in defiance of the ban on language, read as follows:

Dear Comrade Leader President Chief,

We the undersigned (there were no signatures) want to express our concern about survival. We felt secure when we were just O'Kay. But then we became the Republic of O'Kay and you did away with the Republic. When we became the Democratic Republic of O'Kay. you did away with democracy. Now that we have become the People's Democratic Republic of O'Kay, we fear you are going to do away with the people. We would just like to go back to being O'Kay.

Of course the Ruling Council destroyed the letter and adopted a non-verbal resolution denying the letter's existence. However, citing exceptional circumstances, the Council did prepare a reply, using laser beams, which if translated into language would have read as follows:

We don't want to go back to anything. We are a progressive society. Our past was feudal, our present is futile and our future is apocryphal. Happiness is a perpetual Five-Year Plan.

The reply was buried in a time capsule along with an oil painting of the Leader addressing the Cult of Personality.

The abolition of language has gone on now in the People's Democratic Republic of O'Kay for about seventy years, ever since the gains of the Revolution were consolidated. During that period, political science has employed high technology to determine newer and newer ways for detecting violations of the ban on linguistic activity.

One violation, in fact, is the existence of this narrative. Thus, those of you who read it, regrettably, are under arrest.

* * * * *

1988

Full Disclosure

The woman on the screen came after me with no warning. She bounded across the rows of chairs and landed solidly in my lap before I had the slightest chance to react, to run.

Of course she was naked, as most women in pornography films are, except for a pair of mesh stockings, wired for sound, and a concealed camera. And of course the photographers JUST HAPPENED to be there as she embraced me, smelling of anchovy essence and vanilla extract.

It didn't matter that she, that we, did nothing during those few seconds. Nor that she went as quickly as she came, almost before I realized what had happened. For there were no pictures of her as she hurried back to her astonished mate on the screen, in order to climax the scene. No, the only pictures taken were the ones you saw in your local newspapers of the two of us, interlocked.

There is more to the story too, but first I want to clarify my position on a few related issues:

- I enjoy pornography as an art form only;
- I am against all censorship of films, books, or ambitions;
- I do not regard women as sex symbols; to me they have many more important functions, such as campaign workers, voters, consumers and domestic conveniences;
- I am not a degenerate or an aspiring actor.

In point of fact, I am first and foremost a politician, and proud of it. In the days when those pictures were taken I was a fund raiser.

The Party was in financial trouble at the time. Neither Broadway shows, nor sporting events, nor $1,000-a-plate dinners could raise the necessary funds. Campaign costs, particularly for bribes and psychotherapy, were increasing. And so - it was my idea, I gladly take credit for it - I arranged for a private showing of one of the latest "adult" films.

It was an astonishing success. In lieu of popcorn, we provided souvenir handkerchiefs and rosary beads.

The following week we held another showing. This time we even induced a few of the leading objects in the film to make personal appearances afterwards in a back alley to autograph portraits, financial reports, leg casts, and supergraphic dart boards.

We arranged several performances for women only, basically to prove nothing.

The rest is history. In the last election, our Party placed several former film stars in office. In numerous State referenda, voters overwhelmingly endorsed the desirability of massage parlors and male bonding.

Perhaps the greatest irony in the present situation is that the photos you have seen don't even provide a good likeness of me. My face is clearly hidden. I could easily have denied that it was me. Please understand, therefore, ladies and gentlemen of the press, that it was only my desire for full disclosure that prompted me to hold this news conference.

That is the whole truth, so help me God.

—Thank you, Mr. President.

* * * * *

1988

Monkey Business

It was the monkey business that finally did it, that pushed Rudiger Holz from his precarious limb and made him want to drag down the entire petrified tree.

He felt he had to take a stand. He could no longer be a monkey that saw, heard and spoke no evil. He might have been descended from an ape but he would not descend into apedom. He was determined to resist having to correct an error that had not been made.

What the Russian wanted was for Holz to "correct" the summary of a statement the Russian had made during a debate on human rights, and which had appeared in a press release prepared by one of Holz's staff. Holz was the Chief Editor of the Central News Section at One World, the world's largest political organization, headquartered in New York City. The Russian wanted Holz to issue a corrected summary that would rephrase some of what he had said - which he claimed had been distorted - and would also add to his statement more than a page of something he had *not* said.

Like any editor, Holz instinctively resisted issuing corrections because he felt they reflected unfavorably on his operation. If a delegation insisted, however, he would comply and try to make the correction as short as possible.

But on this occasion he felt he was being asked to go too far. Besides, the business about the monkey was absurd.

At first Holz had been prepared to negotiate with the Russian in order to appease him, even to add a few phrases that had not been spoken, if needed to clarify what *had* been said. But then the Russian insisted that the maxim about the monkey be included in the "correction", a maxim he had never uttered: to wit, "Even a monkey can fall from a tree".

At that point Holz refused. And that was when the trouble began.

* * * * *

The Russian, Ivan Golov, came to see Holz the day after the human rights debate had taken place. The two men were studies in contrast. Holz was tall, thin and blue-eyed, with a shock of red hair and a full, bushy red beard. He was West German by birth, having been born and raised in a suburb of Munich, but he was American by adoption, in mannerisms as well as attitudes. He rarely wore a tie, and spoke English with a broad, American accent that he had picked up while going to college in Pennsylvania. He had spent most of the last twenty-five of his forty years in the United States. His movements were graceful, athletic. He always looked as though he had just walked off a squash court or out of a sauna. He was also a closet beatnik. Middle-class respectability, whether Teutonic or American, had never been his ideal. He made his concessions to convention in much the same perfunctory manner as he made his concessions to issuing corrections in press releases, but beneath it all he was a romantic rebel. He hated all organizations, One World included. But he was neither violent nor vile in his opposition. He was not a bomb thrower. He was an emotional anarchist, a poet of the impossible, a dedicated iconoclast, a student of the absurd. He was a cartoon in the body of a man.

Golov, on the other hand, was an *idee fixe* in the body of a man, a Marxist-Leninist secular priest, a self-righteous political goon who offended everyone, including his own Soviet colleagues, with his crass self-promotion and relentless opportunism. Unfortunately, he had high political connections in Moscow and could not be easily ignored. He was tall, heavy, blond and awkward. He had tiny brown eyes inside a puffy, pinkish face, and arms that hung down like plumb lines. He smoked constantly and was short-tempered and apoplectic. He was a constant complainer. He complained about interpretation services, he complained about documentation, he complained about parking facilities, he complained about the weather, he complained about American imperialism, and he complained about press releases. At thirty-five, he felt that one way to advance his diplomatic career was to complain. That way, in addition to being noticed, he might also gain a reputation for being a perfectionist.

"I must have a correction," he told Holz the day he came to see him. "Your press release missed the essence of my speech, and you didn't give me the space I deserved." Press releases were the unofficial summaries of official meetings at One World. Each day members of Holz's staff would attend the meetings of various Committees throughout the Organization and write summaries of the debates at those meetings. Although the summaries were intended primarily to assist journalists in filing their stories, delegations frequently sent copies to their capitals to show their Foreign Ministry what had transpired at a particular meeting.

Holz asked Golov where the error was.

"During the debate on Honduras I made a major policy statement about American imperialism in Central America, and the importance of bananas. You gave me only five paragraphs in your summary, and only two sentences about bananas. You can't split the two issues. Anyone reading your summary would think I was a..."

"Banana split," Holz volunteered.

Golov ignored Holz's comment, concluding: "...a fool. And you left out the part about not learning from history. It was the most important part of my speech." Golov tapped lightly on the desk with his fist for emphasis.

Holz had a copy of the press release on his desk. He leafed through it. "On average, every speaker got three to four paragraphs; you had five. If we gave you any more, other delegations would have complained we were favoring you. Besides, we have to be concise. You know we can't cover every point in a long speech." He paused. "But we did pay attention to your bananas," he added,

"Two sentences on my bananas. Do you call that attention?" Golov asked. "No, it is not enough. Besides, I've decided to add the following phrase. It will make my argument even clearer: 'Even a monkey can fall from a tree.' Do you understand? The imperialists wander in the jungles of Central America and think they understand the needs of the people. But they are monkeys. And even a monkey can fall from a tree. That is one of the lessons of history. Clever, eh?"

Holz started to cough and almost choked. Embarrassingly, Golov had terrible body odor.

"Well?" Golov said.

Holz wanted to scream. Instead, he picked up his copy of the press release again and carefully bracketed, in red pen, two sentences about the lessons of history and two more sentences about Golov's goddam bananas. He then handed the release to Golov to look at, to prove that his points had already been summarized and that there was no need to issue a correction.

But Golov ignored it. "I have read your press release. That's why I'm here," he said.

Holz nodded. "But did we make any *factual* errors?" he asked.

"There were errors of judgment. There was an intentional distortion," Golov said. He lit a cigar. It smelled worse than he did. Holz, who was not usually sensitive to smells, tried to breathe through his mouth.

"That's a very serious charge, sir. We have no political bias here. We are international civil servants and we are objective. There was no *intentional* distortion."

Golov gushed smoke. He was wearing a light gray suit that looked as if it had just come out of a washing machine, and a thick cream-colored tie that looked as if it were made of plastic. Fashion is decadent, subtlety is bourgeois affectation, his image said. "Tell me, Mr. Holz, what was the nationality of the press officer who reported on my speech?"

Holz tore at his bushy beard. The vulgarity of the question offended him bitterly. How often in this Organization, he thought, matters of intellectual substance were reduced to a question of nationality, race, religion - the lowest common political denominator. And though the Soviets were not the only ones who did it, the Soviets always did it. "It's not relevant," he answered, breathing through his nose again, and regretting it.

"And you. You are from the Federal Republic of Germany, is that right?" Golov continued.

"Yes, I'm German," Holz said, purposely avoiding saying *West* German.

"I see," Golov smiled, as though he had made a clear and incontrovertible indictment.

Holz twisted in his chair. "Mr. Golov, I understand your objections. But what you're asking for are additions, not corrections. Could you please tell me if there were any *factual* errors in our coverage?"

Golov pulled two typewritten pages out of his briefcase, and handed them to Holz. "This is the correction I want issued. Put this out and we'll have no trouble." He stood up to leave. "And don't forget about the monkey falling from the tree," he added.

Holz's mouth opened wide. "But..."

"It's all very clear," Golov said, walking toward the door.

"But wait. You understand that I can't promise anything until after I've read this, and then listened to the tape of the meeting to see if there are any discrepancies between this and what was actually said.

And then we might want to make same minor stylistic changes. I'm sure there won't be any problems..."

But Golov didn't want to listen. He was already on his way out of the office, trailing smoke and malodorous charm. "Goodbye," he said.

Holz turned and opened the window wide. The stink was pervasive.

* * * * *

Golov had come to see Holz on a Thursday afternoon. On Friday morning at 10 a.m., Holz was at the door of Jan Nordvik, his immediate superior, who was the Director for Media Relations.

Nordvik was a tall, thin, gray-haired Swede in his fifties, whose main interests were horticulture and the advancement of his career. Between writing books about flowers and tending to the indoor and outdoor gardens at his home, he socialized with delegates and media representatives, trying to keep everyone happy. His enemy was controversy. He didn't care about substance, morality, justice, or personalities. He wanted the people he dealt with to like one another.

He was also an ex-diplomat who had been placed at One World because his Government no longer wanted him in its Foreign Service. He had been in the Swedish Foreign Service for twenty years but had been forced out for being an alcoholic, and because of an indiscreet affair he'd had with the son of a high-level European diplomat.

He had not, however, left the diplomatic corps without means of recourse. Considering the amount of intimate information he had collected while in the world's rotten capitals, he made it known before submitting his resignation that he wanted a high-paying sinecure at an international organization, or else he would write his memoirs. He already had a book contract in his briefcase when he went to see the Foreign Secretary with his proposal. Negotiations ensued and a deal was struck. Nordvik was installed as Media Relations Director at One World, whereupon he agreed, in addition to resigning from the Foreign Service, to end both his drinking and his bachelorhood. A month after joining One World he married a woman many years older from an influential French banking family. Though his homosexual liaisons continued, he gained a respectable, and prosperous, social partner. And he stopped drinking.

As for his book contract, he converted it to another volume on horticulture, entitled *The World of the Pansy*.

Holz didn't like Nordvik. He didn't like him in principle and he didn't like him in practice. He considered Nordvik to be part of the growing diplomatic trash pile that was taking over One World. Governments were constantly "dumping" at One World diplomats they could no longer use themselves. Holz was against that in principle.

In practice, he was against Nordvik because he considered him a "cave man", a man who caved in to all outside complaints about the News Section, regardless of merit or origin, in order to keep the peace. Therefore, he had little hope when he went to see Nordvik that Friday morning that Nordvik would agree to oppose Golov's request. Yet, Holz knew he had to see him.

"I just can't issue a correction," he told Nordvik after he had explained the particulars of the complaint. "It's a travesty. Corrections are one thing; clarifications are one thing; but lies are something else. And this stupid adage about a monkey, which has no relevance..."

"Wait," Nordvik interrupted. "Ours is not to interpret relevance. Our job is to report."

"On what?" Holz asked cagily.

"On what was said - with some background and amplification, if necessary."

"The monkey was not said. The monkey did not happen. And it has no political significance whatsoever."

"Rudiger, you have been in the Organization longer than I have. You know the political significance of keeping the super-Powers happy," smiling. There was a brilliant display of pansies - violet, sunshine yellow, and white with red centers - stunningly arrayed in a wide-mouthed, white vase on Nordvik's window ledge.

"There are other obligations besides keeping the super-Powers happy. There are things like integrity and pride."

"I can see you're still a young man in spirit," Nordvik said. "The Organization needs men like you."

"The Organization needs an enema."

"What?"

"The Organization has enemies, and its enemies are undermining its effectiveness."

"The Organization's effectiveness consists of serving its Member States. If it loses their confidence, it can no longer be effective."

"Golov isn't important. He's just a low-grade infection. We could ignore him."

"Golov is more important than you realize," Nordvik said. "He has some very influential friends."

Holz tore at his beard. Nordvik glanced at his flowers. "There must be some compromise we can make, Rudiger, isn't there?" Nordvik said after a few moments.

Holz reached into his briefcase and presented his first concession. "I stayed last night after work and listened to Golov's actual speech from the official tape of the meeting. It was in Russian, of course, but I got a friend of mine, who's a translator, to transcribe it for me in English. Here's a copy for you. Here, also, is a copy of our press release, with the passages, which I think are adequate, about Golov's bananas and the lessons of history. And here's a copy of the two-page 'correction' Golov wants issued. Now, I'm prepared after having read all this material to issue the following five-line paragraph, as an addendum, not as a correction. I think it should satisfy the Soviets."

Nordvik took the four documents and laid them in the middle of his desk. "I knew you were a sensible man," he said. "Sometimes, after all, the most important thing is to be practical, don't you agree?"

"Impractical," Holz said.

"What?"

"I'm practical," Holz said.

Nordvik smiled again. Then he read Holz's proposed addendum. "You've left out the monkey," he said.

"*He* left out the monkey. You can read the transcript of his speech."

"Very well. Let me examine these documents and I'll get back to you," Nordvik said.

"Yes, sir," Holz said. As he left, Nordvik's secretary was calling to him: "There's a Mr. Golov from the Soviet Mission on the phone for you, Mr. Nordvik. He says it's important."

* * * * *

Luis Marengo, the Mexican who produced the press releases on a mimeograph machine in a large room down the hall from Holz's office, was not at all surprised when Holz asked him to stay a little late that Friday night to run off a correction - after he had printed out all the afternoon releases, and presumably, after everyone else had left the office. What did seem a little strange to Marengo was that Holz asked him not to deliver the 500 run-off copies upstairs to be distributed among journalists. "Just leave the copies on the table next to the machine," Holz told him. "I'll take them upstairs myself when I come to the office Saturday."

Earlier that afternoon Nordvik had called Holz to his office to discuss Golov's complaint. "I think Golov has a point," Nordvik had said. "The press release was adequate so far as it went, but Golov explained to me that his statement was more than just an intervention on the topic of human rights in Central America. It was a statement of Soviet foreign policy *vis-a-vis* the Third World as a whole; so, on that basis, some extra space would be justified. Don't you agree?"

"If he gets more space, others will want more space. Delegates count lines, whatever the substance. Our press release was accurate."

"I know what you're saying, and in other circumstances I would support you, but in this instance Golov is willing to go to great lengths to press his case. He is prepared to go all the way to the top of the Organization, and I don't want that to happen. I don't want it to appear that I can't handle my own Division."

"He won't go to the top. It's a bluff. Only the head of the Soviet delegation can go to the top."

"Golov can make it very unpleasant for us. He can tell his Ambassador that the press officer was an American..."

"How did he find out the press officer who wrote that release was an American?"

"He found out."

Holz grimaced. He suspected that Nordvik had volunteered the information.

"He can claim there was political distortion and that this is just one more example of how media relations in the Organization are controlled by Western countries. Individual incidents have a way of building up, and after a while the Soviet Ambassador could make a formal complaint, listing a series of incidents, including this one, and the pressure might increase to place more Soviets in key positions in the Division. It would hurt your career, Rudiger. I don't have to go on, do I?"

"I wish you would." Nordvik, of course, had a key position in the Division.

"Very well, then. I think it's in the best interests of the Division, and of the Organization, to honor Golov's request. At the same time, I can assure you that this correction will not in any way reflect on your performance as a professional."

Holz stood up and walked around Nordvik's office, admiring the wild and stunning displays of flowers. For the moment he felt he was in a botanical garden of the spirit, a perfumed respite from the jungle of endless political machinations. He respected Nordvik's passion for flowers. "Can we call it an addendum instead of a correction?" he groped.

"No, I think we'll call it a correction to avoid the suggestion that he's adding something new. We'll just add the paragraphs Golov wants. That should be easy enough, don't you think?"

"No, it won't be easy. It'll be a disgrace."

Nordvik frowned. "But you'll take care of it, won't you?"

"I'll work something up. I'll try to condense what he gave us, and then I'll show you the result." Holz chewed on his lip.

"I think it would be safest just to print what he gave us," Nordvik said, returning to Holz the papers Holz had given him that morning.

"Do you mean, print as a correction everything he gave us without dropping a word?"

"Well, that way there's no danger of a new complaint, since we already have his approval."

"I see," Holz said.

"And don't forget the monkey," Nordvik said, grinning. "For some reason Golov is very serious about that."

"Sheer nepotism."

"What's that?"

"Blood is thicker than water. The Ape Kingdom always looks after its own."

"I don't understand."

"Forget it," Holz said, and then left, perhaps angriest of all that Nordvik had refused to comprehend his humor.

From Nordvik's office Holz went straight to the huge public garden behind the Organization's building. It was a Friday afternoon, and not many people were there. Trying to clear his mind, he wandered up and down the lush and sensuous rows of elegant blossoms, each labeled for its genus and its contributor. In spite of New York City's foul air, an incredible aromatic sweetness pervaded, and the pure colors shone through the afternoon smog like beacons in a storm.

He recalled a day he had once spent at Giverny, Claude Monet's country estate, and how he had left Monet's magnificent gardens feeling that he had been taught to see again; remembering how, unexpectedly, he had been able to recognize five or six shades of green in the shrubbery along the roadway outside as he had begun his hike back to the train station at Vernon. He had not noticed those different greens on the way *to* Giverny. And now, some of that same revelation, rejuvenation, perhaps it was passion, seized him as he gazed at a varied array of violets - most of them African. Though he had passed them by before, today for the first time he became aware of the subtle hues of purple there, six or seven gradations of rich luxuriant petals atop thick, leafy green stems. They seemed to insist that there was an esthetic dimension far beyond the arena of the obvious, a dimension not merely of luxury, but of vital necessity, a dimension that defined individuality.

He continued to stroll among the flowers for a long time before he returned to his office. Then, after doing same routine paper work until everyone else had left, he prepared the following "correction", which he gave to Luis Marengo to produce on the mimeograph machine.

"In the press release of ___ May, the following paragraphs should replace paragraphs five and six of the statement by Ivan Golov of the Soviet Union:

"Western imperialists have entangled themselves in the jungles of Central America without realizing the true nature of the struggle there. They are like monkeys chasing after rotten bananas. But there is no tree they can climb, however tall, that will give them the proper perspective on the future, so long as they covet their so-called pluralistic democracies. Nor will those same monkeys be able to find a tree strong enough to resist being uprooted by the inevitable conflagration of totalitarian socialism.

"What the Soviet Union wants in Central America, as everywhere else in the world, is to make local Governments subject to the aims of Soviet foreign policy. Those who resist Soviet objectives and the inevitable triumph of socialism are like monkeys hanging from a dead tree. And we must never forget that even a monkey can fall from a tree."

Holz did not place copies of the "correction" in the distribution area upstairs for reporters to see on Friday night, or on Saturday morning as he had told Marengo he would. Instead, he took the weekend to consider his actions. Then on Monday morning before anyone arrived at work he did, indeed, place copies of the "correction" in the distribution area. By 9 a.m., he knew, the journalists would be reading them.

And at 9:30 a.m., as soon as Jan Nordvik arrived at his office, Holz was there to present him with his resignation.

* * * * *

1985

Robogogue

Determined to win the election, the Party assembled a bionic candidate intended to be unassailable, unscrupulous, and unisex. It called him/her *A*braham *W*ashington *L*incoln (a.k.a. AWL, a tool for penetrating the complacent safety belt of the people). The media called him Robogogue.

AWL had several identities, depending on the audience. For the most part, AWL was a black Baptist Minister who had served time at several universities and exposed himself from numerous pulpits. As a man of the cloth, he occasionally dressed in a wet towel.

AWL launched his presidential campaign by burning a cross on the lawn of a synagogue in Cleveland on Yom Kippur, and accusing Jews who protested against his religious activism of being anti-black. In that same address he praised the religious leadership of Iran and accused its critics, as well as his own, of being atheists, and therefore, un-American.

He prided himself on being color blind, and formed what he called a People's Spectrum. He hugged anti-white terrorists and denounced white-collar crime. He denounced anti-black terrorists and hugged blue-collar criminals. He embraced red Blacks and assailed blue Whites.

He manipulated the media to climax.

At the annual convention of PLOP (Palestine Liberation Organization Party), where he received the Golden Kalashnikov Award, AWL advocated lynching enough of the majority race in each State until each State achieved an ethnic balance. "The democracy of Lebanon must be our guideline," he said.

AWL's uncompromising crusade for equality also led him to advocate AIDS infections for chronic heterosexuals. He proposed setting up a viral transmission center (VTC) in any neighborhood with an excessive disbalance of heterosexuals, and infecting them selectively, the project to be paid for by a special tax on the children of unbroken families. "Only if them gits what the others got can we all come together," he said. AWL received immediate support from the Gay Condom(inium) Community (which advocates gay cohabitation without condoms).

"A virus ain't got no color," AWL told a nationwide television audience when questioned about his proposal to erect a viral transmission center in Foggy Bottom.

"Which means what?" a reporter asked.

"Which means that all Queens have genes, and that equal opportunity means equal opportunity."

"Will you ever cave in to public pressure?" the reporter asked.

"I am not a cave man. That is a racist remark," AWL replied, ending the interview.

During a three-part debate against other Presidential hopefuls, AWL appeared during the first part as a Lesbian Palestinian terrorist, targeted by Israeli 'straights', during the second part as a Hispanic cocaine smuggler harassed by racist police, and in the third part as an illegal alien refusing to learn English. Whatever his identity, however, his proposals were consistent. His main platform was: "Gimme!"

At the end of each intervention, a crowd of his supporters would chant: "Gimme! Gimme! Gimme!" His campaign slogan was: "Gimme AWL You Got!"

The greatest obstacles in AWL's campaign for the Party's nomination were the other candidates. Thus, he set out systematically to destroy them, with a policy he termed RILT (Rumor, Innuendo, Lie, and Threat).

AWL's leading rival was a white man from New Mexico, whom AWL accused of being racist for not having been born Navajo. In a series of television spots, accompanied with background music by Stevie Wonder and financed by a philanthropic Libyan mental institution, AWL chanted: "You white, me black. You like whiteskin, me like redskin. You demagogue, me robogogue." Although a CBS/New York Times survey later showed that most of the American electorate (by this time, 75% functionally illiterate) didn't understand what AWL was saying, they liked his rhythm. Soon after the ads began, AWL's rival withdrew from the race, confessing during a press conference that he was a "humanizer" (i.e., interested in human beings rather than votes), and that it was too late for him to change his style now just to be elected.

Another of AWL's rivals was an off-white, widowed Congresswoman with a long record of being controversial. She believed in putting criminals in jail instead of in charge of social programs, in teaching English in the public schools, and in paying athletes less than soldiers. Once again, AWL went to the air waves to appeal directly to the people, this time dressed in drag and posing as a rehabilitated talk show host. He threatened to preach in her neighborhood if the Congresswoman didn't withdraw from the race. Of course she withdrew, and the media praised AWL for his warmth and honesty.

Through a "leak" to the news media, yet another rival was proven to have connections with organized crime, because his fourth cousin twice removed had once lived in the same city with the third cousin once removed of an alleged Mafia chieftain six times removed to Sicily. Robogogue's ads in this case went (with musical background by a millionaire folk singer who professed to hate money): Would you buy a used child from this man? (Both the video producers and the newspaper that broke the story won professional awards that year.)

AWL's most controversial proposal, however, came at a Veteran's Day celebration honoring the American brain dead who had perished in the country's wars against learning foreign languages. Dressed in a red, white and blue turban and a Cuban army uniform, AWL demanded that Congress enfranchise all illiterates, worldwide, in order to create a better political balance in Washington between the know-nothings and the do-nothings. All the major television networks immediately supported him. The Book Burners Association made him a lifetime, ex-officio, good-will ambassador.

The Congress, reluctant to enfranchise foreigners, struck a compromise by adopting a strong bill encouraging and subsidizing domestic illiteracy. In addition, the omnibus Orwell Factor bill made it a federal crime not to be a member of at least one recalcitrant minority, or not to have demonstrated hatred for authority in at least one public forum.

Months later when AWL captured his Party's nomination, he chose for his vice-presidential running mate an orange-skinned civil liberties feminist ("Agent Orange", he affectionately called her) who had become rich defending bisexual anti-American terrorists. The Party closed ranks behind the ticket. "Gimme! Gimme! Gimme! Gimme AWL You Got!" supporters chanted.

In his first address after winning his Party's nomination, AWL called for amnesty for productive capitalists and individualists of all races, and advocated federally financed programs to retrain non-bureaucrats in memo writing. He proposed legislation to declare logic an environmental hazard.

In another speech AWL promised to fly to the Everglades, if elected, and give the vote to alligators, who were being terrorized just so white ladies could have fancy pocketbooks. Reacting against programs to institutionalize homeless schizophrenics, he proclaimed them an endangered species, and argued that they had as much right to sleep on sidewalks as the rich had to walk on them.

Meanwhile, the major opposition Party nominated a person who could read, speak and write English correctly. The pollsters gave him no chance of winning.

Robogogue appears to have won the minds and hearts of the mindless and heartless. His supporters come from all sidewalks of life - self-hating Americans, avaricious anthropoids, democratic decadents and intellectual innocents. And everywhere one goes, one hears the rhythmic chant, or sees the red, white and blue posters and advertisements proclaiming: "Gimme! Gimme! Gimme! Gimme AWL You Got!"

The results of the upcoming November election are a foregone conclusion.

* * * * *

1988

The Contest

An ingenious friend has left a note on my desk. No, actually, it is a contest application of sorts.

It is a piece of paper, at the top of which is scotch-taped a headline from the financial pages of the New York Times: "U.S. Gives Seoul a Textile Ultimatum".

Then beneath the pirated headline the following instructions appear:

CONTEST RULES: In twenty-five words or more, compose a convincing story to go with this headline.

PRIZES: The winner will receive a signed copy of his own story, plus three other stories he might have written if he had not written his own. Second prize will be nothing.

DEADLINE: No entries will be accepted after the contest has closed.

Two entries, unsigned, were attached to the original note. (I suspect they were written by my friend.) I have decided to call them A-1 and A-2.

A-1: A rare fourteenth century ultimatum, one of the first such diplomatic documents known to mankind, was presented by President Nixon to the South Korean Government today, as a special gift. The ultimatum was written on a multi-colored cloth of woven silks.

A-2: The United States warned today that unless the South Korean Government voluntarily restricted its export of cheap textile products to the U.S. market, the United States would be forced to retaliate with massive raids by B-52s.

The difference in tone between these first two entries reaffirmed my belief that beneath every humorist there lurks a shark. I shall not comment on the weighty significance of the fact that the harsher entry came AFTER the comedy had been dispensed with; suffice it to say that I myself preferred A-2. (Apparently I was to be the final judge of all submissions.)

Within minutes another entry was hand-carried to my office. I shall refer to this one as entry B.

B: The ultimatum recently given to Seoul authorities by the United States Government was revealed today to have been based on false information. President Snee Kee said he had evidence that the U.S.

document was a "complete fabrication", and essentially nothing but a "textile ultimatum".

Other entries followed, and since space is limited, I shall list only those with limited space.

C: The United States sought today to ease relations with city officials in Seoul, who were outraged last week when textile ultimatums were sent to every South Korean municipality except the capital. The U.S. embassy in Seoul blamed the mix-up on postal delays, and hurriedly rushed another copy of the coveted ultimatum from Washington by air courier. (Accompanying photograph shows U.S. Ambassador smiling and shaking hands with Seoul Mayor as he presents him with document.)

D: The world's largest collection of textile ultimatums, to be exhibited in Seoul, Korea, at the 1974 International Conference of Coercive Documentation, was increased by one today when the United States presented the South Korean Government with a white bedsheet purported to have been worn by the founder of the United Klans of America. "Get Out Of Town By Sundown" was stencilled across the sheet.

E: The dispute between Washington and Seoul concerning the best material on which to issue ultimatums took a new turn today when the United States presented the South Korean Government with a textile ultimatum. Embroidered in red velvet, the ultimatum carried the seal of the ILGWU, and contained instructions in the Korean language to the effect that diplomats who did not report for duty on Sunday would be required to turn in their credentials on Monday.

One entry was in the form of a letter.

F: Dear Mr. Contest Judge: I've been trying to write a story that would play on the word Seoul - you know, Seoul food, Seoul brothers, etc. - and imply that racism was reflected by the misspelling of such an important word; but I couldn't put it all together, if you know what I mean, so I thought I would just submit the idea itself, for what it was worth. Perhaps I could get a partial prize, half credit, or something like that. Dig? (The letter itself was full of misspellings, which I have corrected.)

Then there was an entry that was really more of statement than a submission.

G: It's smart asses like you who are undermining the credibility of the press with your intellectual games and snide insinuations. For anyone who was well informed, the meaning of the headline would be quite clear. The ambiguity only exists in your warped, Commie mind.

(The rest of this entry was unprintable. Oddly enough, I liked this one.)

That night I analyzed the entries - there were about 20 in all - and discovered some fascinating consistencies, in spite of the varied backgrounds of the entrants. Without exception, the entries were:

1. In some form of English.
2. Either signed or unsigned.
3. Indicative of a sophisticated understanding of political journalism.
4. Written by people proud to be Americans.

(I must confess I submitted at least two entries myself.)

The next day I awarded the prize. It was only coincidental that one of my entries won.

My friend, incidentally, who is even more just that I, agreed completely with my decision. "The acorn does not fall far from the tree," he said.

"Man is a political animal," I replied.

We preserved the results of the contest in a manila folder marked "Contest" and filed them in a drawer marked "Files".

I am a winner at last.

* * * * *

1973

News Junkie

My friend called to say he had just heard on the BBC that World War III had begun.

I switched on the TV to Network News I. Lead story: how many Christmas presents were being returned this year as opposed to last year. Next: favorite mixed drinks over the past 12 months. Next: the growing market for hair transplants.

I clicked over to Network News II. The newspersons were giggling about the weatherperson's tie and assaulting the English language. Next: advertisement for deodorants with French names. Don't be the last one on your block to smell like an American. Then, a review of the latest Oliver Gallstone movie about the CIA/FBI/Pentagon/Wall Street plot to prevent America from being converted to Islamic fundamentalism, gay pride and repackaged democratic socialism. Docudrama at its best, the reviewer said, using ventriloquism to speak through his asshole.

More news: an in-depth interview with a bisexual fashion designer reflecting on unisex hairstyles, transvestite chic, and the gender-specific nature of freedom in Japanese bordellos. Followed by a feature story on endangered tundra in baked Alaska.

I called back my friend. He was listening to the French news. World War III was in full swing. The President person was preparing to address the American people.

I turned on to Ted Turn-on of CNN fame, Time's Man of the Year, Jane Fonda's man for the Week, and Saddam Hussein's PR agent. A panel of intellectuals was eulogizing Mikhail Gorbachev for having tried heroically to save Communism. Mohamar Khadafi was being given a Doctorate of Humane Letters at Harvard.

I switched to All-News Cable Channel I, determined to find a newscast. The newspersons were conducting a phone-in poll: how many sausages can Madonna swallow without gagging? The viewer had only to dial the appropriate 1-900 number to indicate his/her/its/their choice.

Next item: a cross-country march by black Hispanic lesbian AIDS patients protesting whatever they were not. Followed by a feature item: live interview with an ACLU lawyer outraged that serial murderers did not have tile bathrooms in their cells.

On to Network News III. Alas! A 10-minute advertisement by shouting salesmen for gas-guzzling American cars. Naked nymphs telling why every manperson should have a hot rod; three-piece suited weasels waving American flags; politicians demanding campaign contributions; bogus road tests in the Nevada desert; smell of burning rubber; patriotic harangue about the need to support home-grown mediocrity. Cartoon of Japanese car salesfox being impaled on an American car radio antenna.

Pause. Another advertisement: Preview of new talk show by Reverend Off White, to be broadcast direct from federal prison where the Reverend is serving time for having looted funds from several Government-sponsored projects. "Ah done thought that self-help meant to help yourself to as much as possible," sayeth the Reverend. "But now Ah realize dat what it do mean is for all lawyers to help theirselves."

And then a break in the action. When we come back, we'll have more, the blue-eyed anchorette promised, on the recent massacre at a California fast food outlet by a renegade Malthusian distressed about the prospect of global detente. Followed by an editorial commentary on the prospect of reconvening Middle East peace talks in a Brooklyn delicatessen.

Ah, the news! My condom for the news!

My friend called again. He was listening to the Swahili news. World War III was still pumping away. Millions being killed. Cities being destroyed. Nuclear threat.

I switched to All News Cable Channel II. A ceremony was about to begin on the canonization of an American correspondent who had made live broadcasts from a bunker in Baghdad during the Persian Gulf War. "Thank you, thank you," the correspondent said in accepting the tribute. "I only wish I might have been around to do the same for Hitler during World War II. He should have been allowed to give his side of the story too. After all, the American Government was (chuckle, chuckle) controlled by a certain ethnic group that was not exactly *sympathetic* to the Nazis. And the American people never had the chance to hear the other side. Maybe Jews and Gypsies and Slavs *were* a little difficult for the German people to accept. Who knows?"

And so on.

Wonderful! the Media Czar in charge of the ceremony cackled. Give that courageous journalist two prizes. One for Baghdad and one for Berlin. Then, a spontaneous homily on the meaning of adversary journalism. To be a successful American journalist one had to doubt one's origins, one's Government, oneself. If one could not be adverse, then one could be perverse. But never objective. That would only play into the hands of the dreaded Normals. To be a good journalist one had to assume that anything pro-American was a lie.

Back to Network News I. Giggling. Sports. More giggling.

My friend called again. He was listing to Ashanti News. The former Soviet Union was falling apart. Civil war in Yugoslavia. There was *news*!

On to Network News II. In-depth interview with a female womanperson on why there should not be gender-specific language and why the word "lesbian" should be capitalized.

A male man called in to tell Ms. Guest that he felt men had been victimized in the Persian Gulf War. If she believed in gender nonspecific equality, and if more than 50% of the U.S. population was female, then why had 50% of the U.S. combat soldiers in the Persian Gulf not been female womanpersons?

Msteak, replied Ms. Guest. That's like saying that only 12% of professional basketball players should be black.

My friend called again. He had been listening to Yoruba News. Nuclear weapons were being aimed at the U.S. World War III was getting dangerously close.

I turned back to Network News I, which was showing a replay of the 1948 World Series.

Network News II was airing a talk show, hosted by a retired college football coach who was learning to read. The coach was interviewing a successful narcotics dealer who had made his way out of the ghetto by keeping his neighbors in the ghetto. His other guest was the current holder of the Ms. Moronic Cupcake Award, who was suing Mike Tyson.

"Why are you suing Mike Tyson?" asked the interviewer.

"Isn't everybody else?" she replied. Smiling. Showing leg.

"Did you ever have intercourse with him?" came the discreet question.

"My attorney sez I did," replied Ms. Cupcake.

"Do you know who Mr. Tyson is?" interjected the millionaire Narco.

"You're just trying to penetrate me because I'm a woman," came the reply, smiling; revealing pubic hair.

I turned on All Cable News Channel III. Crimefighters. A weekly show with the latest statistics on violence. Re-enactments of violence. Photos of violence. Sex crimes. Muggings. Contest for Sadist of the Year Award.

My friend called again. The President person was about to address the nation.

Back to Network News I. A special on how typical Americans were coping with the burden of being Americans. Four specimens: an unemployed gayperson who had been assaulted by a pit bull in heat; a recent Guatemalan immigrant who spoke no English; a black serial killer serving a life sentence; and fourteen-year-old Vietnamese orphan dealing heroin. Being atypical, I switched off.

Network News II. Movie of the week. Interesting script, except that since every other word in the film was considered obscene, and had to be excised, there was no sound track. And since nudity on screen was prohibited by God, there were no pictures.

Anyhow, I watched the dark screen for a while, until I could no longer control my curiosity for the news. Then I switched to Cable News Channel I, with a roundtable discussion on whether or not history existed. Very high-powered intellectual heavies debating: Ms. Professor A of the Testosterone Alert Center, who insisted the topic be referred to as *her*story; Mr. Professor B of Alternative Lifestyles Foundation, arguing that straight history was not the same as gay-lesbian history; Mr. Ramsey Clark, in a three-piece camisole, arguing that America was not part of history; and an anonymous orang-utang under contract from Random House for $6 million to write a new history of evolution.

My friend called again. He was listening to Wolof News. The American President person was trying to address the nation, but was being interrupted every fifteen seconds for instant analysis by Sam Donaldson.

Back to Network News I. The male co-anchorperson was desperately searching for cliches to describe the terror in the newsroom. War is hell, he kept mumbling.

"The first casualty of war is truth," his co-anchorette said.

"History makes strange bedpersons," the co-anchor male person said.

"War is hell!" the co-anchorette added.

"I said that already," the co-anchor male person said.

"But it's the first time I said it!" co-anchorette replied, alleging sexual discrimination.

"Ha! Ha! Ha!" weathercreature chuckled.

"I *love* your hair," the sportscaster said to the blond-haired anchorette.

"Ha, ha," came from everybody. Wasn't this fun?

I heard explosions outside. Switched to Foxy News. Queen Gertrude was doing a number on Hamlet. The Kennedy family was balling the entire Peace Corps. Elizabeth Taylor was getting married to a stray she had picked up in Toys R Us.

I prayed to the ghost of Mark Twain.

Back to All News Cable Channel I. A Leninist pre-analysis of what the U.S. President might say. Followed by a feature commentary by an ex-football coach on the lack of sympathy for varsity athletes who couldn't count past 10. (Captioned in black English, with cartoons for the mentally impaired.)

I switched off my TV. Called my friend. No answer. The explosions were getting louder, closer.

Not much time left, I feared.

* * * * *

1992

Banana Politics

It was during the air war against sigatoka, over the lush jungles of Central America, that I first learned about the intrigues of banana politics.

I was flying low and alone in my unarmed, twin-casket, swing-wing Messerschmitt, spraying lethal chemicals and dodging phalanxes of hostile grasshoppers, when suddenly a giant banana appeared on the horizon, its green skin like a brushstroke against the clear sky, and a deep, male voice boomed: "Help. We are all brothers under the skin. Save me!"

The tropical sun can play strange tricks on a man, so I quickly elevated, invoked a spell I had learned from a United Fruit Co. guru, made a 360-degree turn, and swooped down again from a different angle to see if the experience would repeat itself.

This time a great tarantula appeared on the horizon, its furry legs hanging down like streamers from the sun, and a high-pitched, unmistakably feminine voice said: "Yanqui, go home. Take your money and run."

The fact was that I had been internationally recruited to defend a friendly authoritarian government against subversion by an Asian communist regime that was trying to destroy the banana production of Central America in order to prevent people from getting high on smoking banana skins. Bananas were becoming competitive with poppies, it seemed.

I was being paid well, but I did not consider myself a mercenary since I was completely apolitical, as well as asexual. As a perennial existential bombardier in search of new targets, I had been having difficulty feeding my fantasies, shedding identities, and keeping up with installment payments on my underground shelter. Thus, when an IMP representative (International Monetary Predators) approached me and asked if I would like to earn some quick cash fighting sigatoka, I felt it was my patriotic duty to accept. I thought he was speaking about a rebel Marxist political movement.

Actually, sigatoka is a soil disease capable of destroying an entire banana crop. The name comes from an eleventh century Oriental despot who had a liking for bananas, and once tried to cross the Pacific in a canoe made of banana skins. More recently, the term became a code name for a Vietnamese guerilla leader in the war against rice substitutes.

When I returned to the airport that day and tried to tell the natives about my experience, they became very frightened. They referred me to my flight kit, which contained a manual translated from the Quechuan, entitled *Fear of Flying*.

Then, an Indian boy with twelve toes gave me an amulet in the shape of a phallus to guard against evil spirits, and the local parish priest gave me an immaculate deodorant spray used to prevent tropical hallucinations and to neutralize sacrilegious olfactories.

The air traffic controller, who was on strike, advised me to visit a masseuse in Quito who treated sexual dysfunctions. Unfortunately, none of those remedies worked. I was still confused about whether to continue.

And so, as during other critical periods in my life, I crawled into my orgone energy box, and emerged with these verisimilitudes:

1. Hallucinations are like vaccinations; they protect you from mortality.

2. Once you start a job, you should finish it, more or less. Once you start a life it will finish you, more or less.

3. To understand banana politics, you must solve the following riddle, which drove Nietzsche mad: *Warum ist die Banana krumm*?

Suddenly, the chime on my digital wrist watch went off, and I knew I had to act.

I reloaded my twin-casket, swing-wing, Dionysian air buggy with lethal chemicals and filled my pockets with sugar-coated gumdrops. This time I took a co-pilot with me, named Mother's Day. She was a beautiful young mestizo who had won international recognition by devising extreme goals for which children could compete in order to satisfy their parents' ambitions.

We climbed into the sky as though it were ours, and swept down over the diseased soil and sprayed mercilessly. Once again, an enormous green banana swelled on the horizon and beamed messages in our direction. But we ignored him. And once again, a gigantic tarantula spread her furry legs in all directions, virtually swallowing the sun and emitting warning signals, but we ignored her too.

I popped a gumdrop.

Mother's Day was wild with excitement.

"What are we doing here?" she asked, wild with excitement.

"Do you mean, why are we doing *what* we are doing here, or, why are we here at all?" I asked. I am very particular about language, especially when it is used for communication.

"Exactly," she said. Her hand groped instinctively for the joystick.

"We are doing what has to be done and what we have been paid to do," I said.

"Then why are you so frightened?"

"Because I am not a banana," I said.

"Nor am I a tarantula," she said, caressing the joystick.

"You don't understand. One should not risk one's life for what one is not," I said gravely.

She laughed and laughed and laughed. She was having a wonderful time. A swarm of locusts arrayed themselves playfully off to the left.

Mother's Day continued to play with the joystick. I sprayed again and again. I felt like a killer, but I was enjoying it tremendously. I began to compose verses about dealing death to sigatoka. ("No soil will foil what toil hath grown. Die, sigatoka! The yellow skin will do you in, sayeth the djinn. Die, sigatoka!")

We cruised above the tree tops and outstretched arms of the banana bushes. I knew my mission was either crucial or irrelevant. If the banana crop could be saved, the Government would remain in power. But if sigatoka were victorious, then foreign trade with foreigners would suffer, inflation would inflate, blood would run in the cowpaths, and the Government would fall.

I sprayed and sprayed. Mother's Day manipulated the joystick vigorously. I swore an oath to do something historical one day. Legions of locusts fell before my mighty sweeps.

The soil rose up in tribute. Mother's Day said she loved me.

I could taste success, and it was sweeter than I had ever imagined it could be, once it was peeled.

I flew several missions that day. And each time I landed for refueling and a new supply of gumdrops, the banana growers shouted encouragement and offered sacrifices - goats and pigs and political critics. As a special tribute, the President of the Republic presented me with a key to the Amazon jungle.

Once it was clear that I had won the battle and conquered sigatoka, my old friend the air traffic controller - who was still on strike and had retrained himself as a religious architect - templed a glorious erection in my honor, thereby consecrating my victory.

Ernest Hemingway dedicated a posthumous bullfighter to me.

Months later, when a new banana crop burst forth and soil tests showed no sign of sigatoka, the ruling military junta got high on banana skins and named a cocaine field after me.

Today the Republic's economy is stable once more. Torture has regained its prominence in internal affairs, censorship of the press has been restored, and women have been ordered to cover their heads, eyes, ears, torsos, legs and fingernails. Banana poachers are hanged by the toes until bitten by a tarantula, or they are quartered and buried under whipped cream and crushed nuts.

As for my own fortunes, of course I did not work for nothing, and with the money I earned I built myself a comfortable, eight-bedroom tree house in southern California, with a private jungle, a meditation plantation, and an orgone energy box for each third day of the lunar cycle.

I have retired from mercenary activity completely, and am considering a career in politics. As I told Mother's Day recently - she lives with me now - I know what I know, and what I know is bananas.

"Exactly," she said.

* * * * *

1982

Poet

My friend travels light: a comb, a toothbrush, a razor, and a condom. Because he is a poet, he also carries pen and paper.

The paper is white toilet paper. White, because that color coordinates with almost any other; and toilet paper, because he wants his few supplies to have as many uses as possible and because he wants to be able to dispose immediately of any bad poem.

So far as I know my friend has never written a bad poem. So far as I know he has never written a poem of any sort. But, as he says, writing is not the issue for a true poet. Most important is the vision. Then, with a minimum of technical facility anyone can write a poem.

And, in fact, the minimum technical ability needed is becoming less and less. Poets can now win prizes for being able to fill out contest forms correctly. A grant was awarded last year to a poet in residence at the Pre-School Educational Foundation for being toilet-trained.

As for my friend, last year was a particularly creative one for him. He went through two million rolls of white toilet paper.

Although he has not yet written a poem, my friend already has his spiteful critics. The Environmental Protection Agency hates him, the Oral History Association considers him dangerous, and Plato's ghost wants him expelled from the American Republic.

To add to his problems my friend has met a woman who has fallen in love with him for his poetry. She is a beautiful woman, very romantic, and had always wanted to fall in love with a poet.

Some women love doctors; some, politicians; some, businessmen; and some, poets.

Who can understand women? Who can understand poets? Who can understand love? Who can understand anything?

My friend decided, after meeting this woman - her name is Virgin Forest - that he would compose an epic poem about the origins of evil, to be written in Pascal (a computer language, as well as a French cultural relic).

Virgin Forest believes in my friend and has supplied his every need, from combs to paper. Not since the 10 million member Nation of Islamic Diarrheals descended upon the corporate offices of Scott Paper demanding preferential treatment had such a massive amount of toilet paper been assembled as was assembled by Virgin Forest on my friend's behalf.

I said it was unfortunate that my friend had met a woman who fell in love with him for his poetry. I should explain. My friend wanted to be loved for himself and not for his poetry. My friend feared Virgin Forest had a different idea of poetry than he had, and that, therefore, she loved him for something he was not. He didn't ever want to feel that he had to write a poem or had to remain a poet, in order to keep her love. He didn't ever want to feel he had to achieve anything in order to be loved. In fact, my friend was not even sure he wanted to be loved, since it involved too much responsibility for him.

Once my friend told me he thought of love as an unwritten poem. He clutched fast to his toilet paper when he said that, I remember.

My friend's early research into the origins of evil began with a detailed examination of rusted amino acid chains and rotten apples. He formed a research organization called Amino Apples, applied for a grant to the Ford Foundation and was soon off on his merry way with an apple orchard and the undying devotion of Virgin Forest.

My friend confined his studies to evil as manifested in the human species; he didn't know if it even existed in other forms of life, on other planets, or in other dimensions. Nor did he care. And, since he was convinced that evil caused decay, physical as well as moral, he believed that by examining decayed specimens such as rusted amino acid chains and rotten apples, he would have a better chance of isolating something significant, perhaps even himself.

He recorded his findings daily in religious parables which he then programmed in Pascal and punched into a bisexual Apple computer named Gene Splice. When I asked him why he used so many symbolic names, he told me he was a poet and that, therefore, I should mind my own goddam business. And he showed me a copy of his poetic license, complete with self-portrait and social security number.

The preface to my friend's epic was expected to run about twenty four volumes. It was to be password protected at all times, since my friend did not want his epic read before it was written. Besides, he feared that if someone were to access Gene Splice and decipher his religious parables, it would be tantamount to opening Pandora's Box. Evil, after all, was not something to be taken lightly. It was highly contagious, potentially lethal, and could have the effect of a love potion.

Ever the poet, my friend was fond of saying: Those who knowingly search for evil are likely to find it. Or, again: Those who do not knowingly search for evil are also likely to find it.

Although my friend's fame grew as years went by, his lifestyle remained humble. He continued to eschew all possessions except for a razor, a toothbrush, a comb and a condom. He slept naked, except for a curse that he wore around his waist, in the cab of a pick-up truck that he named Beelzebub. In the truck, meanwhile, he carried only Gene Splice, a month's supply of toilet paper, a gross of disposable pens, and Virgin Forest.

My friend's search for rotten apples led him at one point to a garbage pail at a bordello in Marseilles, where he found that the rats were complaining they couldn't eat rotten fruit because it smelled like a British prostitute. Shortly thereafter, my friend heard a trout off the French coast complaining that the fauna he dined on were not using the proper perfume. He also met a Greek oceanographer who was threatening to sue the Atlantic Ocean for being the wrong temperature.

It was on the basis of those experiences that my friend then developed an important understanding of the nature of evil: it was relative. In France, for example, it was equivalent to bad food. In Germany, it was any form of disorder. In England, it was poor pronunciation. In Nigeria, it was the neighboring tribe. In America, it was dirt. In Saudi Arabia, it was the Renaissance. In Israel, it was the rest of the world. In China, it was human fertility. In India, it was humility. And so on.

From there my friend developed the understanding that not only was evil relative, but also that relatives were evil. In fact, more misery comes from one's relatives than from any other source, he was fond of saying.

As for his work on defective amino acid chains, my friend spent years searching for missing links to explain how homo sapiens evolved from the primal soup, but he got nowhere. (He called his chains *Macho Man* and *Ms Woman*.)

"All my chains turned to noodles and my primal soup samples turned to gruel," he lamented to me one day. "I had to conclude, therefore, that evil was environmental and not genetic. After all, could evil possibly exist without an environment?" he asked.

"No," I affirmed. "Nor could an environment exist without evil."

When my friend had completely finished his research, he did two things: he destroyed his computer and he married Virgin Forest. One of those two things, he confided in me, was pure evil.

Meanwhile, my friend has still not written his epic poem. Or any other poem.

As for myself, I shall miss my friend, who now lives on a dirigible and speaks to no one. In truth, I have no other friends, and I was in love with Virgin Forest for a long time. She once told me, in fact, that I might have had a chance with her if only I had never written a word. Of course I understood very well what she meant; for I, too, am a poet.

* * * * *

1986

Note for the File

This story begins on 1 January 1984, when I received a mailing from Buck, Buck and Dollar Literary Agency.

The letter read:

Dear Author:

As you can appreciate, the cost of processing literary items has been increasing precipitously of late. Our research indicates that over the last decade alone the total cost for publishing and marketing a book-length manuscript of 300 pages has risen 500 per cent. And, there are approximately 35,000 books published in America, every year, along with *tens of thousands* of magazines, newspapers, newsletters and trade journals!

There is too much being written. There is too much being published. There is too much being read.

As a recognized leader in our field and consistent with our responsibilities as good corporate citizens, we are taking a two-pronged initiative to do something about the flood of written words, and of literacy, which threatens to submerge the very foundations of our society. We would like to offer you an opportunity to join us in our effort.

First, we are urging you to participate in a concerted letter-writing campaign to Congressman Gorgon J. Morgan of Utah, to encourage him to sponsor a bill that would place a heavy tax on all non-utilitarian writing - such as poetry; novels of ideas; sacrilegious satire; obscenity; pornography; pro-abortion, left-wing or right-wing, do-good, soft-hearted, unilateral-disarmament-type propaganda; and any criticism of Motherhood.

Second, we are offering at an introductory bargain rate, to provide you with a unique service that will reward you for not writing any longer. If you sign the enclosed card and return it in the stamped envelope provided, we will guarantee that nothing you submit for publication will ever again be printed.

This is how our service works:

1. You will be assigned a number - coded to reflect your age, sexual preference, ethnic background, voting record, blood type, political opinions, and liquid capital.

2. That number will be entered into a computer (which we call "Gutenberg"), with the main unit and comprehensive memory bank located somewhere in a cave in Utah (Congressman Morgan's home State).

3. A complete list of ex-writers will be sent, free of charge, to all publishers of everything.

4. Whenever you submit a manuscript (anywhere!), your code number will be fed to Gutenberg. Your name will then appear, with a red line through it, on the computer screen of the publisher, and your manuscript will be immediately shredded, thus saving the time and expense of editors, printers, distributors, readers, and so on.

There was more, too - 6 typewritten pages in all, including 4 annexes.

Annex I contained a list, by topic, of what might be considered non-utilitarian. Annex II contained a list of writers who might be considered non-utilitarian. Annex III contained a draft version of the bill that Congressman Morgan was being asked to introduce. Annex IV contained a list of everyone with a non-American surname.

The letter was signed by the President of the Agency, whose name I at once recognized. He had recently sold the rights for a television serialization of the life of Theodor Herzl to a Saudi Arabian banker for $100 billion in gold, a Harvard Business School degree, and a night in a heated swimming pool of his choice. As part of the package, the Saudi also holds an option to purchase the European Renaissance, as seen through the eyes of The Beatles.

Once I survived the initial shock of this letter. I sent the following reply in the stamped envelope provided:

Dear Buck, Buck and Dollar:

&*$%+*?#!

(signed) John Doe, Esq.

Two weeks later I received the following from Buck, Buck and Dollar.

Dear Author:

Thank you for your positive response to our offer. You are among over 100,000 former writers who have signed up for your service. Enjoy!

(signed) R. Fullerton-Roxbury Blah

President, Buck, Buck and Dollar

Enclosed was an invoice: $15 for the first month of service, and $20 for every month thereafter for the first year. If, within the next week, I signed up for two years, the rate would be less. An accompanying card also warned that by next year prices might go up. Finally, it was possible to contract for lifetime coverage, which would also entitle me to a gift: the complete works of William Shakespeare, shredded; or the memoirs of Eve Peron written on an IUD.

A second enclosure was a form letter to Congressman Gorgon J. Morgan of Utah, urging him to introduce a bill along the lines mentioned in the Agency's first letter; I was advised to sign the letter and mail it in a stamped envelope marked *confidential* to an address in the Bedford-Stuyvesant section of Brooklyn, from where it would be forwarded to a post office in Utah.

I ignored this goddam, stupid mailing, which I considered to be an assault upon my privacy. I threw the entire package in the garbage.

Within the next ten days, however, no less than seven of my manuscripts were returned - shredded. Only my name was left intact, with a number next to it that I took to be a code.

Then, two weeks later I received another letter.

Dear Author:

WAIT A MINUTE! When you agreed to employ our services, you undertook a financial obligation. Our records show you are in arrears. Please send along your payment in the enclosed, stamped envelope, so that we will not have to refer your name to our legal department.

There was also an application to join "The Former Authors Society". A list of charter members of the Society was on the masthead, most of whom I had heard of: Virgil, Dante, Chaucer, and so on. Except for Martin Borman and Richard Nixon - both recently restored to political respectability, but neither of whom I had ever considered an author - the charter members were all deceased.

Three more shredded manuscripts of mine were also returned.

Finally, there was an application for honorary membership in yet another group - STAFIL: The Society to Stem the Flood of Literacy. A promotional pamphlet, entitled "The Flood of Literacy and What You Can Do About It", spoke of the disincentive of teaching people to read, which would then discourage them, and others, from writing, which in turn would limit the amount of published material. The slogan of STAFIL was "There is too much being written. There is too much being published. There is too much being read."

The pamphlet was, actually, very clever. It presented excerpts from published material that was, by anyone's standards, atrocious. Since prohibiting the publication of such trash might run into opposition from "First Amendment anarchists", the argument went, the most effective way to prevent publication would be to limit the number of people that could write, and inevitably, that could read. The right to read was not guaranteed by the Bill of Rights. (Major television networks, the pamphlet indicated, were eager to support the campaign to discourage literacy.)

Although no dues were required for an honorary membership, contributions were solicited.

Of course I was outraged by the proposal, but since I wanted to keep in touch with STAFIL, I decided to become an honorary member. I figured I could use their material somehow; it was too unusual to ignore. I sent along a check for $50.

Days passed. A few more shredded manuscripts were returned. Then I received a telephone call from a man identifying himself as Arduous McGinty, legal counsel for Buck, Buck and Dollar. It was about my overdue account, he said. He cajoled, then threatened. He did not want to have to obtain a court order to attach my salary, but after all, I had contracted for certain services, and I was obliged to live up to the terms of my contract. I told him to put it all in writing.

And, indeed, he did put it all in writing. At which point I made a photocopy of his letter and sent it, along with other correspondence on the case, to the Consumer Protection Agency. I had had enough. I also returned McGinty's letter, shredded.

But three days later, I received shreds of my own letter from the Consumer Protection Agency (of which McGinty was a trustee), as well as a more vigorous and nasty threat from McGinty. Oh, yes, in McGinty's envelope was another application - for membership in a secret society of book burners (acronym: BOOBS).

I realized that I was up against a formidable opponent. There were other developments over the next few weeks, but they are not worth detailing, except to say that they followed the same pattern. Every effort I made to defend myself was frustrated, scorned, defiled. The threats became more ominous. I appealed to the New York Times, the President of the United States, and the Worldwide Wrestling Federation. My hopes were shredded each time.

I soon understood that I could not win a court battle either. I had neither the time nor the money to confront Buck, Buck and Dollar. Besides, how could I afford long absences from my job as a witchhunter to appear in court?

So I paid. After all, money talks and it is polyglot. I paid for protection. I paid for peace of mind. And at first, I even tried to look on the bright side of the deal I had made: no more worries about rejection slips, no more haggling about payments, no more bickering with editors, no more neurotic concerns about creativity.

But after a while I had second thoughts. Although I had paid, and was still paying, I realized I could never capitulate psychologically. Instead, I decided I would use my ingenuity to make the situation work to my advantage. Writers must be practical, not romantic.

And so, in a determined reversal, I became active in STAFIL and became a charter member of BOOBS. At the same time, I constructed an underground printing press and continued to write, produce and store my own manuscripts, thoroughly undeterred by the fact that I had no audience. Who needed an audience anyway? I had a dream, America, I had a dream.

Besides, the number of unread writers has always exceeded the number of those who are read. It is a grand tradition. As someone must have said: the unread are the true tongues of the race - or at least, the mandibles.

Now, a year later, I personally account for seventy percent of the published literary material in the United States.

(Incidentally, my printing press and storage facilities are fully automated, use subterranean water power and are nuclear blastproof.)

As literacy continues to dwindle, my production soars.

I shall not be satisfied until I am the only published writer in the nation.

* * * * *

1984

Of Births and Birthrights

A few years ago I was fortunate enough to become a father for the first time. I even saw it happen. I was in the delivery room. I filmed the birth. The pictures came out. I had proof that my daughter was born.

But the Bureau of Vital Statistics would not accept my proof. Perhaps they had a deep mistrust for the Truth, as presented by Eastman Kodak. Perhaps they were chronic skeptics, or worse: baby haters; family planning, abortionist, godless atheists; spies for Polaroid. In any case, I had to fill out a form with detailed information and apply for a birth certificate. I even sent a $5 check and asked for additional copies of the Truth in print, which apparently took precedence over the Truth on film.

But three months later I received an empty envelope from the Bureau. I recognized my own handwriting on the front; it was the same self-addressed envelope I had sent along with my check and the proper forms three months earlier. Obviously there had been a mistake.

I sought wisdom in the friendly telephone directory and called the appropriate number. A recording answered - a slurred, bored voice that suggested I call a different number for the proper information. I did what I was told. I was determined that my child should enjoy the benefits of her birthright.

The telephone rang for five minutes without an answer. I hung up and re-dialed. Still no answer. I assumed that I had called either in the midst of a tic-tac-toe tournament, a two-hour coffee break, a fire drill or a union meeting. No matter; one had to endure, a child's identity was at stake. Finally, a heavy voice, no recording, answered: "You've got the wrong number, buddy. That recording is wrong. We've been meaning to change it." I was given yet another magic number.

This time the voice was cordial, and the instructions detailed. I was told to: write a letter explaining what had happened, have that letter notorized, enclose the original empty envelope, ask for a new set of forms to fill out, secure a statement from the physician who had attended my child's birth...and so on, there was more; not forgetting, finally, as with all governmental transactions, to include my social security number.

"Who? What? Where? When? Why?" I demanded.

"Oh, with a problem like yours, mister, maybe you'd better come down here," the voice said.

I went. A journey of beautiful journeys: tunnel of love to Worth Street, disembarkation at the architectural splendor of Brooklyn Bridge, and ascension up the stone steps to daylight, a dry birth of sorts. Then the excitement of staking out a trail to the immortal Bureau of Vitals, at last to confront the bookkeepers of history with their flawed handiwork.

I demanded satisfaction from the receptionist at the Bureau. She directed me to an arrow which eventually directed me back to her desk. "Last door on your right at the end of the hall," she said the second time around.

"Which end?" I said.

"That one," she said, and waved me toward an intersection.

I wandered lonely as a cloud. A large room filled with signs and people challenged me. I stopped in front of a sign that said MAKE SURE TO GET IN THE RIGHT LINE.

But there were no signs above the booths themselves, so that angry knots of trusting souls were inevitably forced to stand on line to find out where they should stand on line.

HAVE YOU FILLED OUT THE PROPER FORM? another sign said. But as with the first sign, there was no telling which form had to be filled out until one waited in line to find out which line to wait in to find out which form to fill out.

"Only a poet would appreciate those signs," said a man standing next to me.

"I'm sure they *mean* something," I said.

"One can never be too careful with disclosing official Government information," he said.

I noticed a door at the end of the panel that separated the people from their dedicated servants. I watched and waited. Occasionally the door opened. I shot through it at the first opportunity.

A woman looked up from her desk. "Yes, mister?"

I revealed myself to her.

"The certificate's probably been lost," she said. "You see, we put the folded certificates in an envelope, and then send them down to the mailroom to be sealed and stamped. There, they shoot through a machine. If the certificates aren't folded correctly, they fall out of the envelopes onto the floor. And down there in the mailroom it's all kids, the new generation. They don't care. They're always messing up. You can't get good civil servants any more, believe me. If you want to know the truth, this new generation ain't so damned good, no matter what *they* think."

I agreed.

She asked me for the date of my daughter's birth.

"Aha!" said she. "That means the certificate would have been mailed out during this week," pointing to a calendar.

I didn't know what to answer.

"I was on vacation that entire week."

"Oh."

"Don't you see? That means somebody else folded that certificate."

Another exclamation of surprise from my astonished larynx.

"I understand it all now. It's quite clear what happened to your daughter's certificate," she said, with a Conan Doyle flourish.

"But?..."

"Somebody *folded* it wrong!"

"Wow!"

"Here, let me show you how to fold these things correctly." A lesson followed. "Now you try it."

No sacrifice too great for a proud father. I folded.

"You're very good, mister. You'd make a good civil servant."

I mumbled my gratitude for the compliment.

"Tell you what, mister. Do you have a few minutes? I'll go down and look on the mailroom floor. Maybe it's still down there. They don't often clean the floor."

I waited. She returned in a matter of seconds. "There's nobody down there now, they're taking a coffee break. The door's locked."

A wry smile. "Why don't you just let me fill out another form? We'll start all over again."

Pensive. "All right," said she of desk 4. "You'll have to fill out *this* form, reaching for a paper among piles of papers, and bristling with professionalism.

"Can I do it here? *Now*?''

"No. You'll have to take it home with you, and you and your wife will have to sign it in the presence of a notary.''

"A *notary*?"

"Yes, don't you know what a notary is?"

"But you can't expect me to drag my wife and three month old baby around the neighborhood looking for a notary just because your mailroom messed up!"

"Well, *she* (looking at desk 3, adjacent) won't accept your application unless it's signed by a notary. That's the first thing she looks for."

It was then that I uttered those desperate words that are the last resort for all who assume themselves to be worthy of special consideration: "Let me speak to your supervisor."

"It's *her*," pointing once again to desk 3, now empty.

I mumbled my thanks and promptly claimed the empty chair abutting desk 3.

Now I have worked for government organizations myself, and I am not unaware of the confusions that sometimes occur in large bureaucracies. Yet I am also aware of political intrigue. And so, in those few minutes while I waited for the resident of desk 3 to return, I began to dream wildly of what might have happened to my good daughter's certificate. Perhaps it had been pilfered, to be used eventually by some international crime ring (I had read *Day of the Jackal*); or perhaps this foul-up was an insidious form of population control - not that it would discourage pregnancies, but that it would result in falsifying statistics (which are more important than facts), and thereby officially limit population growth. Or perhaps it was part of some sexist plot. And on and on. The mind, as Marianne Moore once said, is an enchanting thing, an enchanting thing, an enchanting thing...

In any case, the resident of desk 3 returned a few minutes later. She was a pleasant and gracious middle-aged woman, and was quite helpful. She allowed me to fill out the forms right there, she answered my several questions about the form's questions, and she signed a few times in lieu of my having to see a notary. She told me everything would be all right, and that my daughter would officially exist within another four to six weeks. She even conveyed her belated congratulations for my good fortune.

But six weeks later I had still not received an official birth certificate. So, once more, I made another journey to the Bureau of Vitals. This time, being a veteran, I made no pretense of standing on line with the masses. I merely waited for the right door to open, and shot in like a hero.

Surprise: the supervisor I had spoken to the previous time was not there any longer. She had resigned. Armed with righteousness, I persisted and asked for the new body. It was a man, and he was equally pleasant. I filled out a new form.

Two weeks later I received three official copies of my daughter's birth certificate. My wife's age was incorrect, and my birth place was incorrect. I did nothing.

One month after that, I received three more official copies of my daughter's birth certificate. This time my wife's age was correct and my birth place was correct, but my daughter's middle name was misspelled, and the time of her birth was off by twelve hours. Once again, realizing that I was outmatched, I did nothing.

A few months ago I went to register my daughter for nursery school and was asked to produce a copy of her birth certificate. I couldn't find one. During the past three years we have moved and many of my papers have been lost. Moreover, at this point I don't feel emotionally capable of facing the Bureau again, and so, for a while, things will have to remain the way they are. (The nursery school, incidentally, once it had judged me to be financially solvent, trusted me even without a birth certificate.)

I sometimes think I ought to be concerned as to whether or not my daughter officially exists. For according to the copies I once had but have since lost, the Bureau's official records are, in fact, incorrect. What the legal implication of those inaccuracies means is something I choose not to consider, but which might actually prove to be very embarrassing, if not bizarre. At any rate, I am not a lawyer, nor was meant to be. I only mention the situation out of an inveterate respect for facts.

On the other hand, perhaps it might be better if my daughter did not exist officially. After all, what greater legacy could a parent bequeath to his children than to liberate them from the official records of the State?

Ah, freedom!

1975

The Scrooge Club

I am soliciting members for my Scrooge Club. Everyone is eligible, regardless of age, gender, race, religion, or dendrite activity. There are no annual dues. The only obligation is to protest as widely and as vigorously as possible against the mandatory merriment of the Yuletide season.

Like American Presidential election campaigns, the Yuletide season is being increasingly advanced. Santa Clauses are appearing on the scene even before Thanksgiving (thus demonstrating their lack of respect for territory carved out by the turkey lobby). Apparently, in the Land of Overkill, one cannot begin too early to shop, to be jolly, to shop, to be righteous, to shop, and to be reminded of obligations to family.

There *will* be gaiety. There *will* be gifts. There *will* be spirituality. There *will* be family celebrations. By order of the Church, the Government, and the U.S. Chamber of Commerce. The same troika that brought you Ash Wednesday, The Decline and Fall of General Noriega, and Monday night football has officially decreed Winter Solstice Bliss. Any unhappiness will be legislated out of existence.

There is no escaping the oppressive hyperbole of the Christmas season in the United States. The media gorge themselves on it. One can not pick up a newspaper, turn on a radio or a television set and not be reminded of one's family obligations. To aspire to any element of private choice is to be unpatriotic.

Meanwhile, there are tens of thousands of homeless people with nowhere to go on the putative birthday of Jesus Christ, except to a local soup kitchen; even more who are decent souls but have no families to cradle them, or who lack the funds to afford extravagant gifts. These are warm and modest people who resent being told what to feel and when to feel it. Indeed, to barrage such people with a demand that they not only be blissful, but that they be so precisely in the way authorized by Big Brother, is not simply insensitive; it is cruel.

One of the basic human rights in a free society should be the right *not* to have one's private feelings expropriated. If an alien political philosophy were being imposed on Americans with the same frenzy as the Yuletide yatter, it would be termed demagoguery. But when hypocrisy is cloaked in red and green, and blessed and merchandised by the most trusted, then it becomes the patriotic spirit of the season.

The answer is not to reach out spuriously with sanctimonious glee to the homeless, the indigent, and the non-believers in an attempt to make them participants in a commercial myth, or actors in a national farce. The answer is to leave them alone. Happiness can not be legislated. Nor merchandised. Nor enforced. Let those who want to celebrate do so. And let those who want to be left alone be left alone.

The Scrooge Club needs your support.

* * * * *

1991

Integrity

I once knew an Irreversible Intellectual. He carried his bowling ball with him wherever he went. The ball was in a black shoulder bag made of Dead Sea scrolls.

Whenever a debate became too practical he would roll the ball right down the middle of the discussion group, or across the table top, knocking off arguments like pins.

His integrity was a weapon. His bowling ball could be wrathful.

But like many intellectuals he liked his creature comforts. And so, each finger hole in his ball was lined with fur. Meanwhile, his palm generated sparks when he delivered an opinion, so that there were many days when he smelled of singed fur and righteous perfume.

Bad grammar was to him a sign of incompetence, an unforgivable transgression. He had the letters BG emblazoned on his ball.

When I first met him he was rolling against the collected works of Jean-Jacques Rousseau, whose optimism he considered to be impure because Rousseau had abandoned his children at birth. In similar fashion, he denounced Marxism because one of Marx's daughters had been a suicide.

He bowled over television tubes on principle.

He challenged national identities, he disputed traditions.

He became a crisis.

I was appointed to head a commission to deal with him. But he wouldn't speak to any of our members. All our correspondence, including subpoenas, was returned unopened, with only the letters BG imprinted on the envelopes.

At one point he offered to surrender his bowling ball if in return he might be granted exclusive rights to the First Amendment. I told him he already presumed to have those rights. He immediately bowled over the telephone on which I made the call.

As a conciliatory act I mailed him a bowling alley, complete with pins, an automatic setter, and a self-winding public relations agent. He accepted them.

He named the alley Self. It became a family to him.

He uses it constantly now, and bothers no one any more.

I am a national hero.

1982

Suckcess

In one of my previous incarnations I was a parking meter.

There were several advantages: I had regular working hours, the law was always on my side, I had no sexual frustrations.

For a nickel I could flip my lid.

I was happy.

But as civilization advanced, those of us in the inner city suffered. Neighborhoods deteriorated. Young toughs took to slapping me around for a rotten dime. Stray dogs used me for their business. Bums leaned on me and loitered.

I rusted.

Then came the urban renewal gang and I was offered several options: to be transplanted to a deodorized suburban area; to become a parking permit; to be re-trained as a cash register in a toll booth. I said no, no, no. One did not surrender tradition so easily.

I also rejected the idea of becoming a garage, even a high-priced one, because I couldn't stand the thought that any strange vehicle that could pay the price could enter me.

Most of all I didn't want to have anything to do with time-keeping any more. I'd had enough of setting limits for people, and of spying on innocent vehicles. I wanted to be timeless.

Then about a decade ago, following a long and acrimonious Congressional debate, I was selected to be a space station. The competition was severe: an empty lot, an underground garage, a pushy laser beam - and me. I won.

Now people on earth talk about me. Scientists look up to me. Astronauts need me.

Suckcess.

* * * * *

1986

Book of the Dead

What I did was this: I traced the book, through a series of footnotes, to several magazines where portions of it had earlier appeared. The magazines in turn referred to document numbers in an enormous computer with terminals in several countries. The memory in the central unit contained entries dating back to pre-history, apparently programmed by a race that is now either extinct, or has evolved to such a high degree that we are unable to monitor their communications. The question of originality was academic. It was assumed that everything worth being said had already been said at some point in time, even if the proper document number could not be found. That was not the reason for my search. The reason for my search was to preserve pre-history, to protect if from time-warp saboteurs who could destroy the present by altering the past. Unfortunately, I failed.

* * * * *

1986

Ex-Husband In Trunk

The other day as I was driving home from work I saw a sign in the back window of a woman's car: "Ex-Husband in Trunk". Being an ex-husband myself, I understood exactly how she felt.

I followed her car. She led me through boulevards named after male athletes and back streets named after Fannie Hurst. Each time she stopped for a red light I could hear sounds emanating from the trunk of the car.

She drove a convertible. It was convertible into a pre-World War II bicycle or a Mercedes-Benz, depending upon the target of her economic affections.

I expected her to live in an elegant residence and I was not disappointed. She lived in a high-rise condominium shaped like a dollar sign, that had been built on two acres of landfill made of grape-flavored peanut butter and junk bonds. On the front lawn were several life-size sculptures of prominent environmental trivialists who had been deeply disappointed by not having been able to protest against a nuclear waste plant being built on the premises.

The garage was a capacious, winding maze with circular ramps on loan from the Guggenheim Museum in New York City. I got lost several times. Once I almost ran down a protest group of dissident minotaurs, sequestered mafioso informers and non-unionized Watergate plumbers. They were wearing sandwich boards with exclamation points on one side and question marks on the other.

I saw faded wall posters with pictures of Aaron Burr promoting his upcoming duel with Alexander Hamilton. The match was to be televised, under a grant from the National Rifle Association, and carried live to the Middle Ages via Three Musketeer Satellite.

I knew that I was in my element, and I was convinced that if ever I found what I was looking for here, I would be able to stop driving in circles and park. And to park, to stop going in circles, can be a great relief for any man. Even more than a relief it can have the force of ineluctable necessity, since it is very difficult to park without stopping.

In any case, a maze is no more formidable than any other environment so long as you know where you're going, and don't bang into the walls. As a famous religious explorer once said, "Once you've found what you want, you'll wonder why you ever wanted it."

And eventually I did find the automobile I'd been following. In fact, it was the only automobile in the garage. Cautiously, I approached. I heard sounds. I tapped lightly on the trunk and a voice answered. "No," it said.

"No, *what*?"

"No, never." It was a male voice.

"I don't understand," I said.

"I know that."

"What I mean is, are you really in there?"

"Are you really out there?" he replied.

"Of course I'm out here, and it's where you should be too."

"Why?"

"Because this is the real world," I said.

"No, never. Real is knowing where you are when you're there. I know very well where I am, and I know where you are," he replied.

I quickly ran to check the trunk of my own car to make sure I wasn't inside of it. I saw a tire iron. I brought it with me to the convertible. "Who are you, anyway?" I asked.

"Not important," he said. "Don't bother me with identity questions. I know very well who I am."

"But I don't know who you are."

"*Your* problem."

"All right, I don't care anyway."

"That's better. I'm her ex-husband," he said.

I started to pry the trunk open with my tire iron.

"Hey, what do you think you're doing?" he asked.

"I'm going to liberate you."

"Bug off! I'm already liberated: I'm divorced. If there's anything I can't stand, it's you American imperialists who are always trying to liberate people that don't want to be liberated."

"But aren't you an American too?"

"Of course. Isn't everyone?"

I felt like a foreign object. "But how can you possibly be liberated *in there*?" I asked, withdrawing my iron.

"That's such a stupid question, I won't even answer it."

"Why is it stupid?"

"Because right now, even as you're talking so self-righteously about liberating me, you're looking over your shoulder to see who's watching you."

I looked over my shoulder. A group of homeless people was playing touch football on a far-away ramp. The walls were lined with social workers hiding in shopping bags.

"And," he continued, "anybody who looks over his shoulder as much as you do, isn't liberated. Besides, I wish you would put away that tire iron. I deplore violence. Even if I wanted to be, as you call it, 'liberated', I wouldn't want it done violently. No, never."

"I don't believe you," I said. "I don't believe you're really in there. Are you a recording?"

"Yes, I'm a recording."

"I thought so."

"Did you really? Or were you just hoping?"

"I knew it, I knew it all the time. At least, I suspected it."

"But did you also suspect that I'm a liar?"

I was stunned. I looked over my shoulder again, and then between my legs. "How are you a liar?"

"I lied about being a recording," he said.

"Prove it."

"Do you mean, you want me to prove that I'm lying?"

"Right. Beyond the shadow of a doubt."

"No, never."

I brandished my tire iron like a conquering warrior, and then brought it down heavily on a termite that was crawling on the parquet floor. "Take that, termite!" I said. And once again I appreciated how fortunate I was to have parked my car. Otherwise, I might never have been able to wield my tire iron with such esthetic authority.

"Listen," I said. "Do you realize how ridiculous it is for you to be living in the trunk of a car?"

"Do you realize how ridiculous it is for you to be standing in a deserted garage, holding a conversation with a man who lives in the trunk of a car, and killing a termite with a tire iron?" he replied. "Suppose someone in a white suit should see you now."

I looked over my shoulder and saw tens of men who had been sentenced to death in American prisons, men on death row, wearing white suits and watching me. "Tell me what it's like in there," I said to them. But my friend in the car thought I was talking to him. (Or, perhaps he answered because he knew I wasn't talking to him.)

"I have all the comforts of home," he said. "My trunk is lined with scented fur, and the climate is temperature controlled and dust free. A pearly tube hangs down that dispenses food and drink, and there's a receptacle for me to use when I want to relieve myself. All waste is converted into fuel, so that my ex-wife hasn't had to purchase a single gallon of gasoline since I moved in here. There's light enough to read by, and I can play games on a minicomputer that's also a television set. At first, my ex-wife used to let me out whenever she needed someone to help move the furniture, or carry packages home from Bloomingdale's, or take out the garbage. But that was years ago, before we fixed up the trunk and signed an amendment to our divorce agreement. I can't tell you exactly how long it's been since I was out because I don't have a calendar or a clock, but I remember there were wars going on in several places in the world, and game shows on television, and people were having trouble relating to one another - the usual things, you know."

"I know."

"By the way, pal, what's your name?" he asked. "Just in case."

"Just in case? What's that supposed to mean?"

"Just in case you have one."

"I do have one. But only one. I don't have separate first and last names." And then I told him what it was. "And what's yours?" I asked.

"It's an anagram," he said.

"Which anagram?"

"Any anagram. That's the point. You have to use your imagination. You see, my last name was *Cain* when I was born, but my mother didn't like that, thought it sounded too evil, so she switched a couple of letters and changed it to *I can*. She was an illogical positivist. My father, who didn't like my first name, *Abel*, because it sounded too helpless, switched a couple of letters and called me *Able*. But since *I can* and *able* mean almost the same thing, and since neither of my parents wanted to be mean, they called me *Saturday Night Live* because *live* spelled backwards is *evil* and they felt that living backwards is evil, especially on Saturday night. But that's not my name either because even the most *united* families become *untied* if you only shift two letters."

"You're putting me on," I said.

"All right, Sucker," he said, calling me by my name, "believe whatever you want."

"But what if I should want to invite you one night to a termite roast or a three act word play? How can I communicate with you if I don't know who you are?"

"What's in a name? Just think up an anagram and I'll be there, because I'll always be here. Like I said before, if you know where you are, then you know who you are; and if you know who you are, then it doesn't matter where you are or what people call you. Feel free to invite me any time; that is, if you really feel free and can stop trying to liberate those who are already free."

I realized that I was in the presence of a Master and that there was nothing more for me to say, so I picked up my tire iron and trundled off toward my car. "So long, Anagram," I said.

"So long, Sucker."

The way out was as tortuous as the way in, and I drove like a corkscrew, around and down the winding ramps until my peripheral vision surrendered and I could no longer look over my shoulder. I saw a wall poster saying *Show Me A Sign!*, obviously the work of a degenerate billboard artist posing as a Seventh Day Adventist; but I was in no condition to sign anything, so I kept driving.

At the exit I crashed through a barrier of anonymous achievement lists and found myself on a boulevard named for a male athlete who had been banned from professional sports for refusing to score.

I drove all the way home on automatic pilot and parked my car in an odd lot, determined to be even at last with my opposite number.

As soon as I entered my apartment, I went straight to the bedroom and put a sign on the wall saying HERE, so that in the future I would always know where I was when I was there.

Years later the sign is still there and I am here.

* * * * *

1990

Doing It

Sometimes I imagine killing my psychiatrist.

This is how it happens. I arrive at her office one sunny Sunday morning with my troubles stuffed neatly into a backpack that I carry inside a globe strapped to my shoulders. The globe is the shape of the earth and is filled with the ashes of the dead from every war in the twentieth century, declared as well as undeclared.

(At home I also have a second globe, filled with the tears of abused children, but it is too heavy to carry, at times too heavy even to contemplate.)

I am also carrying a shopping bag filled with dehydrated amino acids, and a few heavy stones named grief and death and injustice and anxiety and guilt. The weight of those stones is tremendous, but I can not leave them behind because it would be like leaving a part of myself behind. Fortunately they are counter-balanced by the load on my back. Finally, because I always carry with me something to read, I've brought along the unpublished confessions of Prometheus, who is a hero of mine. They run to 33 volumes.

My psychiatrist, meanwhile, is quite ingenious, and to provide a diversion for her patients while they're waiting she has hidden and scattered in her waiting room the component parts of an Uzi machine gun. The hiding places are changed every few days. Once I found the trigger behind a wall painting and the barrel inside a table leg. On occasion, the firing pin has been taped to a concealed place in the centerfold of a Playboy magazine.

On the ceiling there is a large target superimposed by a slide projector, and in a trap door under the showcase of brain sections in the corner of the room there is a file of slides that contains a transparency of each patient's mother. At your first visit, you are asked to provide a slide of your mother, along with a physical description of your father and voodoo dolls that represent each of your siblings. The dolls are kept in a wall safe behind a water color of Sigmund Freud masturbating.

If, while you are waiting for your appointment, you should feel the need to be aggressive, you can project onto the ceiling the slide of your or anyone else's mother, assemble the Uzi and fire away. The rubber bullets cause no permanent damage.

On the sunny Sunday of my imaginings I am unusually anxious. I have brought with me transparencies of the few women in my life that I have loved deeply. I adjust the slide projector so that I can superimpose their transparencies, as well as one of my psychiatrist, on top of the slide of my mother. I project them all simultaneously onto the target on the ceiling. With the press of a button, I am able to undress them all.

I can see at once, if nothing else, that the several images don't blend or coincide (to begin with, their breasts are different sizes and shapes), and I'm relieved to realize they are not all like my mother. Apparently, I'm able to love different women.

But the forms are generally too representational, and so I press another button - which is attached to my umbilical cord - and *voila*! the conglomerate transparency becomes an abstraction.

"I am an abstract expressionist of the short narrative," I tell my psychiatrist as she emerges from her office to greet me. "What you see on the ceiling is neither an image nor an ink blot; it is a story complete with characters (the women I have loved), plot (how I won and lost them all), background (my childhood), conflict (me against them), and resolution (the murder I am about to commit).

"You're nuts," she says to me.

"Is that you're as in *you're* or as in *your*?" I ask.

"Word plays are very important," she says to me, trying not to commit herself. Her therapeutic technique demands that she remain as objective as possible.

"Don't you believe that art forms can be interdisciplinary?" I ask. "If plays can be imagined from paintings, if poems can be set to music, then why can't writing be intelligent?"

"I'm not a literary critic, so I can't answer that question. Besides, the abstraction that is supposed to represent me is very unflattering, and shows great hostility to reality. What we should be talking about is the problem you're having with your mother and why you pursue infantile escapist theories, not about your prose style."

"You sound very much like a literary critic despite your denials," I assure her. "But of course you're right about us. Creativity has no place in our relationship."

"Then tell me," she says, sounding very clinical, "how are you feeling today?"

"I reek of mortality."

"Have you had any dreams lately?"

"I'm dreaming now."

"What are you dreaming?"

"I'm dreaming that I don't reek of mortality."

"I think we should talk more about your mother," says she.

"I'd rather not. You see, it took me years to dislodge my mother from my shoulders in order to carry the burdens I have now. Now I carry only the world, which is lighter. For a long time I felt guilty because I couldn't make my mother happy. Now I feel only guilt; I've been able to abstract that feeling, and separate it from my mother. That's what I mean when I say I'm an abstract expressionist. And that's why I don't want to talk about my mother any more. I want to be rid of her."

"Then let's talk about your father." I must tell you at this point that my psychiatrist - her name is Philippa (Phil) Anthropy but she prefers to be called Ms. Anthropy - is a middle-aged woman with prematurely gray hair that she wears shoulder-length. She has a small, flat ass that is not necessarily distinguished, large breasts that are, and an adorable turned-up nose. Her eyes are gray.

"My father is a very successful businessman," I say. "He's quite remarkable, He's made a fortune by fashioning anxieties out of other people's feelings, even though he has no feelings himself - which is also remarkable. He's now working on a slogan that will make every American anxious about being an American."

"It's amazing that you've survived," she says sympathetically.

"But I haven't."

"You've survived the atomic bomb," she says.

"But I haven't! I carry around the ashes of the dead from every war in the twentieth century, declared as well as undeclared - remember?" I say.

"You've survived your childhood," she says.

"But I haven't! At home I have a globe filled with the tears of abused children. Some of those tears are mine," I say.

"You can't continue to carry around burdens that don't belong to you," she says, still in a sympathetic voice. "You must find a practical way to liberate yourself."

"That's what I was trying to tell you, doctor," I answer. "I'm working on trying to abstract my feelings. It's the only way."

She sighs and excuses herself. I have rarely seen her so upset. I hear her in the back office sobbing deeply and changing into a nun's habit. She is really a very empathetic human being. I quickly assemble the Uzi.

She returns in minutes looking very distraught. "I am suffering," she says. "You must help me."

I load the Uzi with a clip of real bullets I have found in the closet behind a photograph of her mother.

"Do it!" she says.

I shoot her again and again and again and again. And then I relax.

I have killed an idea.

* * * * *

1990

Phillip Corwin is the author of a short story collection, *The Way Things Are* (1985), and two books of poetry, *Poems To Keep* (1985) and *Windows* (1990). A graduate of Wesleyan University and Cornell University, he has taught fiction writing at New York University's School of Continuing Education, and has been a Fellow at the Virginia Center for the Creative Arts. He has also been a reporter and editor for United Press International and Barron's National Business and Financial Weekly. His work has appeared in over 65 publications in North America and Europe, including The Christian Science Monitor, The Nation, Washington Post Book World, Contemporary American Satire, G. W. Review, Kansas Quarterly, Kentucky Poetry Review, Pembroke Magazine, and Southern Humanities Review. He is now a political officer with the United Nations, and is a frequent lecturer to student groups and nongovernmental organizations. Recent peace-keeping missions have taken him to Western Sahara, Afghanistan and the former Yugoslavia. In May 1995, he was assigned to Sarajevo, where he assumed the function of United Nations Civil Affairs Coordinator for Bosnia-Herzegovina.